Site Fidelity

Site Fidelity

Stories

CLAIRE BOYLES

W. W. NORTON & COMPANY
Independent Publishers Since 1923

This is a work of fiction. Names, characters, places, and incidents are the products of the author's imagination or are used fictitiously. Any resemblance to actual events, locales, or persons, living or dead, is entirely coincidental.

For information about permission to reproduce selections from this book, write to Permissions, W. W. Norton & Company, Inc., 500 Fifth Avenue, New York, NY 10110

For information about special discounts for bulk purchases, please contact W. W. Norton Special Sales at specialsales@wwnorton.com or 800-233-4830

Manufacturing by LSC Communications Harrisonburg
Book design by Patrice Sheridan
Production manager: Julia Druskin

Library of Congress Cataloging-in-Publication Data

Names: Boyles, Claire, author.
Title: Site fidelity : stories / Claire Boyles.
Description: First edition. | New York, NY : W. W. Norton & Company, [2021]
Identifiers: LCCN 2021004048 | ISBN 9780393531824 (hardcover) |
ISBN 9780393531831 (epub)
Subjects: LCGFT: Short stories.
Classification: LCC PS3602.O9736 S58 2021 | DDC 813/.6—dc23
LC record available at https://lccn.loc.gov/2021004048

W. W. Norton & Company, Inc., 500 Fifth Avenue, New York, N.Y. 10110
www.wwnorton.com

W. W. Norton & Company Ltd., 15 Carlisle Street, London W1D 3BS

1 2 3 4 5 6 7 8 9 0

For Matty,
the reader I love best of all

One way to open your eyes to unnoticed beauty is to ask yourself, "What if I had never seen this before? What if I knew I would never see it again?"

RACHEL CARSON

Contents

—

Site Fidelity

Ledgers

—

WE LET THE DUST settle for a month or two after Pop had his stroke, and then we sold the family ranch all in one piece to a cattleman from Montrose, Henson, whose name Pop didn't recognize. I had been living on the Farallones, studying site fidelity of ashy storm-petrels, birds most people probably haven't heard of and might not ever. An ill-timed oil spill or other catastrophe on the central coast of California could wipe the whole species off the map. It was a plum research gig, every ornithologist's dream job. But I love my pop, so I gave it up and came home. That closing was the only time I've been happy that Pop lost his speech, because I didn't want him to say out loud how much he wished I'd taken an interest in the damn cows instead of the damn birds.

Pop refused to let a subdivision be his last crop, so he gave Henson a good deal. We closed at the end of September. Henson signed the papers with rancher's hands, leathery and sun-weathered, just like Pop's. Henson is my age, plus a few years maybe—divorced, one young daughter—and I'm flat suspicious of the guy. How does anyone in their thirties come out of that recession with the kind of money it takes to buy a quarter section on the river, water rights attached, outside Gunnison?

Pop's stroke stole a lot of things from him that I miss too, some more precious than his ability to manage cattle—verbs, for example, and with them, anything resembling sentences. Also the use of his entire right side and all our savings in medical bills, though that last resolved just fine when we sold the ranch. The worst is that he can't say my name, Norah. Instead, Pop calls me Vera. I've stopped bothering to correct him. Vera, my mother, died in a puddle of her own blood and placenta the day I was born, waiting for the ambulance that turned down County Road 68 instead of County Road 68½.

Pop's not confused the way you'd think. He knows the difference between his dead wife and his living daughter. For the first month or so, he'd wince every time he said it, "Vera," shake his head sadly, look down at his shoes—New Balance sneakers with therapeutic elastic laces, not the boots he wore his whole life. A baseball cap has replaced his Stetson. He's nearly unrecognizable. My friend Julie is his speech therapist, and she tells me that he still thinks *Norah* when he looks at me, it's just the signal gets lost in the aphasic fog that has settled somewhere between Pop's brain and his tongue. When he thinks-Norah-but-says-Vera, it sounds like "Vvvvveera." He gets stuck on that first *v* sound, which, according to the manner of articulation chart Julie put on our fridge, is a labiodental fricative.

"Sounds dirty," I said to Pop. "Labiodental." I adjusted the magnets so I could see the whole consonant chart—the nasals and the alveolars, the voiced and the voiceless.

Pop laughed, and my heart fluttered a little, which I took as proof that it's not broken all the way. When Pop laughs, it feels like we're having a conversation instead of a series of Norah monologues, which are far less graceful than the stories Pop used to tell.

There is no real prognosis for Pop, no clear number of months to live, no percentage of independence he'll regain. Pop appears at once fragile and strong, like an egg. Every morning when I tie his shoes I think, *This might be the last time I tie his shoes*, and also I wonder, *How many more times will I have to tie his shoes?*

I've seen Henson exactly five times since he bought Pop's ranch. I know because I started a page in my ledger just for him. I keep track of a lot of things in my ledger, how often I've turned the compost over, various downy woodpecker sightings, the fact that there were maybe five thousand Gunnison sage grouse left in the entire world last spring. It's a habit I picked up from Pop, the same way I got my head for numbers and my love of Oreo cookies. On October 30, Henson and I nodded hello to each other in the Safeway. He was pushing one of those double-decker small carts instead of a family-sized one, and he was buying cornflakes and vanilla ice cream and other plain, sensible foods. On Christmas Eve, he showed up to church for the first and only time. I swear I caught the candlelight reflect off tears on his cheeks when we all sang "Silent Night," but I can't be sure. By the time the deacons turned the sanctuary lights back on, Henson was gone. He rode a horse in the New Year's Eve parade, his saddle strung with tiny white twinkling lights, and he tipped his hat and smiled at me when he passed by.

The other two times I saw Henson, he didn't see me. I was out birding, well hidden by willow and brush, silent, patient, on the public land that runs adjacent to the west side of our old ranch property, federally managed by the Bureau of Land Management. On March 24, I saw Henson cutting wire on the property line fence that separates our ranch from the BLM land. On April Fools' Day, about a hundred yards down the fence line, he did it again. I got pictures of that one. I went down and checked for new grazing leases, and Henson's name wasn't anywhere. BLM land belongs to all of us and none of us, all at the same time, and grazing it without paying fees is the same as stealing feed. Worse, he'll be sending cattle across Pop's and my secret Gunnison sage-grouse lek in the middle of breeding season, which is just as bad for those birds as a real estate development would have been.

THE GUNNISON SAGE GROUSE have as much to do with the woman I am today as Pop does. In 2000, they became the first new species of bird to be officially recognized in the United States for over a hundred years. I was twelve years old. The whole town was talking about them. Part of our landscape. Part of our character. That kind of thing. I was doing all the ranch chores with Pop by that age, every day a chance to test my courage rounding up cattle, test my strength pulling wires taut on fences, test my stamina working every last hour of light in a day. I knew by the smile in Pop's eyes that he was proud of me, which is how I learned to be proud of myself. In my memory of Pop's voice, he is always saying, because he always was:

Nice work, Norah.
You keep after it, Norah.
That's it, girl, well done.

While we worked, Pop told me stories about his life, before me, on the ranch. My grandmother sucking the poison out of snakebite. My grandfather taking the waters at Waunita Hot Springs. The creamy sweetness of my mother's homemade ice cream. It comforted me to know that Pop and I had other people once. The stories let me blame time and bad luck for the missing members of my family—stop worrying we were alone because something was wrong with us.

The sage grouse had lived on the ranch all along, Pop just

hadn't known, none of us had, that these ones were threatened especially much. The first time I saw them we were out predawn, fixing
the same fence I'd seen Henson cut. The morning was overcast,
sprinkling rain. The sun rose but invisibly, behind the cloud cover,
light fading in by degrees rather than streaming up in oranges and
pinks from behind the east ridge. I heard their calls like bubbles
popping—staccato air-sac percussions, saw the males strutting,
virile. They were so full of themselves, so full of life. I knew I was
witnessing something important and rare. I felt then, for the first
time, the mix of emotions that fragile species have always evoked in
me. Precious awe. A preemptive sadness of loss. Anger and indig-
nation at humanity's deep apathy. Surges of what must be a sort of
maternal protectiveness.

"We'll come back tomorrow," Pop said, "and camp out here
while we get a fence around this meadow. If we can keep it out
of grazing, at least in the spring, we can help save these birds all
on our own. We don't need to tell anyone they're here. Don't need
a government handout to do the right thing. We just need to take
care of our own."

We did care for them. We'd camp there for a week every year,
counting the high males and females, recording the numbers of
viewable copulations (not many), evidence of predator interference
(coyote, owl, hawk, golden eagle). Pop would write it all down in
his ledger.

"It's not a diary," he'd say gruffly, tousling my hair, when I'd
tease him. "It's a ledger. Diaries are for feelings, and I'm not keepin'
track of my feelings. I'm keepin' track of the facts."

Pop kept neat and orderly notes of daily events in a series of
99-cent black-and-white composition notebooks he'd pick up every
year with my school supplies. He was almost famous for the way
he could tell you he sold only 152 head of cattle in 1993, or that the
Blue Mesa Dam generates 60,000 kilowatts of energy every year

while the Crystal Dam only produces 28,000. These days, quantifiers are slippery for Pop and he drops them easily. He can't get his numbers straight at all. It's not a difference in his thinking, just his speech, but it changes everything about how people see him—even how I see him, which makes me ashamed of myself.

Pop's ledgers are how I learned the difference between practical thinking and emotional thinking, the way lots of people who love one way of seeing things have contempt, or maybe fear, for the other. He used to mark my growth on the kitchen doorjamb every six months, copy it into his ledger. If I did that now, to him, I'm afraid I'd find he was shrinking, that the marks would run, gravity-fed, in the wrong direction. Pop writes grocery lists using his left hand since everything that used to be dominant in him is broken. It's like he's in kindergarten, the poor spelling, the shaky, uneven handwriting. Pop wants bananas, Grape-Nuts, and orange juice. He writes: *Bababas. Ceral. Joos.*

There are boxes and boxes full of Pop's ledgers in the detached garage of the old Victorian we bought in downtown Gunnison. His notes from the lek over the past three seasons document a 55 percent drop in the high male population on our land. He never mentioned it before his stroke, and now he won't talk about it at all.

"Pop," I said, dropping the open ledgers on the pinewood table he built the first winter I was away at college, "what happened?"

Pop looked at the ledgers and then at me, surprised, his face tensed, lined. He was my favorite storyteller. Now, he is barely interested in simple conversation.

"Dunno," he said, shrugging his left shoulder.

I tried again. I don't know how much I'm supposed to adjust to this new, more limited Pop, how far I should allow him to recede. "Why so few birds? Is something wrong with the lek?"

Pop was examining his pill bottle, counting his purple morphine pearls, trying to pry the lid off with the thumb of his one working hand. He wasn't listening, or he was trying to look like he wasn't listening.

"Pop," I said.

He shrugged again, then lifted his left hand into the air, annoyed. "Dunno."

Conversations are hard for Pop, but they're hard work for me, too, so much relentless effort to connect, to relate, to love and to feel loved by him. I wanted to yell, to grab his shoulders and shake the news out of him, or at least shake him into being interested in me, in the sage grouse, in anything. But I can't do that. He's my pop, and I love him, and what good would it do exactly?

"Fine," I said. "Boring conversation anyway."

Pop glared at me, hummed a few bars of the Star Wars theme, and ran over my foot with his electric wheelchair as he rolled toward the bathroom.

I DECIDED TO DRIVE out and ask Henson's permission to do the spring count myself, to try to get eyes on the lek. Henson was sitting alone on the porch swing, drinking from a can of Bud in a green foam cozy. A tiny pink bike, the training wheels bent so crooked they didn't sit flush with the ground, leaned against the porch steps, but there was no sign of a child. Henson is a tall man, broad-shouldered, but the way he had his back to the ribboned beauty of the sunset behind him, the way the house loomed dark, surrounding him, the way the porch spread out, empty, in front of him, he looked impossibly small to me. He took another swallow of beer, and I saw a pale strip of skin, tender-soft, right where a wedding band would be. For a fleeting minute, I felt sorrier for Henson than I did for myself.

Henson stood up as I approached. He smiled, but it was guarded. "Norah," he said, nodding a greeting.

"Sorry to show up unannounced," I said. "I didn't have a number."

"All right," he said, motioning toward a plastic Adirondack chair. "Take a load off."

He reached into a small cooler and offered me a beer, which I took, even though I don't much care for beer. I heard an echo of Pop's advice: *When you're trying to sweet-talk someone, Norah, you take what they offer you.*

He asked about Pop. I shrugged. "Dunno," I said.

We sat silently for an awkward minute, drinking beer.

"Feels like you're here to ask me for something I'm not likely to give." He looked at me directly. He had eyes like robin's eggs, blue speckled with brown. They softened the rough of the rest of him. "I've seen the sage grouse out there. I guess you probably want some kind of easement."

My heart sank a little. Not all ranchers are Pop's kind of rancher. Some find these birds obnoxious. Some refuse to pay grazing fees out of some misguided idea about their frontier heritage, about what the nation owes them. Some have organized, call themselves "sagebrush rebels." They've threatened BLM agents at gunpoint. They've invaded National Wildlife Refuges. They've elected sheriffs all over the West who believe the Constitution gives them full rights to ignore federal and state laws. Even Pop, no friend of the feds, thought the sagebrush rebels were a dangerous fringe. If that's who Henson was, I already had my answer.

I took a slow, relaxing breath before I answered him. "I do want an easement," I said, "but I'll settle for access to the land. I'd like to just do a count."

Henson's brow was furrowed. He didn't answer right away. I heard the screech of an eagle and rifled through my bag for my binoculars. I'm never without my bag, my binoculars, my ledger.

Sure enough, I spotted a bald perched in the familiar gnarled old cottonwoods that lined the riverbank.

"Bald eagle," I said. "Want to take a look?"

Henson shook his head no with a sort of bemused expression, like he was indulging a child. It was the same with Pop, who supported birding as a hobby but could not understand it as a dead fucking serious science career.

"They're not exactly rare anymore," he said. "I've been watching that one for days now."

"Sure," I said. "Old news, bald eagles."

"Yeah, you won," he said.

"What?"

"Your people. Environmentalists," he said.

I lowered my binoculars, sat back down. "My people owned this ranch for sixty years. We're not so different from you."

Henson sniffed, looked away. He was right about the eagles. They've recovered. There was a time I found that hopeful, some sort of proof that we humans could still find our environmental emergency brake, as if we'd finally felt the loss of the passenger pigeon, of the Carolina parakeet, of the Labrador duck, of the thirty pages of birds under the Wikipedia category "Extinct Birds of North America," which you don't have to be an expert to google. But not anymore. I'm older and maybe wiser and I know better now. We only saved the bald eagles because we want to see ourselves in them—they are our national symbol, after all, which makes them exceptional in the same way we believe ourselves to be exceptional, the default lens for our worldview. Ordinary birds, like the Gunnison sage grouse, we shrug and let disappear. Which is more proof, if I needed more, that we are not, that we have never been, all in this together.

"Land didn't come with an easement." The sunset was fading.

Henson turned on the porch light. "Which tells me your dad knew better than to invite the government up here, give up good grazing for the sake of some ridiculous birds."

"Pop left that land alone because it was the right thing to do," I said. "He loves those birds."

Henson snorted. "He was dodging the government, or I'll eat my hat. No easement, no mandate. Old ranchers are all the same. You know that. Or you should."

I knocked my empty beer can over when I stood up to leave.

"I'm sorry. I don't really want to say no to you, Norah," Henson said. The apology seemed sincere. "I've put all I have into this place. I won't risk any limited use."

Tears prickled the back of my eyes as I drove back toward Gunnison, because Henson was right, I knew better about Pop. He only saved the birds to indulge me. The minute I left him, he let them go.

SITE FIDELITY IS A beautiful, romantic idea, but it's also dangerous. The Blue Mesa Reservoir filled in 1965, and the following spring a few hundred Gunnison sage grouse descended on the reservoir ice in March, right above where their lek had been, slipping around and falling and failing to mate. The year after, half as many returned. The next year, even fewer, and so on until there were none. They didn't move to other leks, didn't find solid ground on the shore. The entire family just died out, pining for their land.

It's one of the saddest stories I've ever heard, and the first time I heard it, I asked Pop for the same thing I wanted from Henson, to get a conservation easement on the ranch, to give the birds some official, enduring government protection.

"We murdered almost all of these birds before we even

knew they existed," I said. "Building those dams. We have to do something."

"We are doing something, Norah," Pop said. He rubbed his head, which has always been his act of frustration, then he tugged my braid and smiled sadly.

"They need us to do more," I said. "We can do more for them."

"The government can't protect them better than I can," Pop said. "Grazing has hurt these birds, no question, but so did those dams, which the government built. Our birds, Norah, we keep for ourselves, keep secret. That's how we keep them safe in the world."

My pop has always been the North Star of my life. I set my moral compass by his worldview, consider always how my choices will affect his good opinion of me. I see Pop's heart for ranching and his heart for the environment, and I'm grateful for the clear land ethic I learned at his knee. Pop read me Ed Abbey and Aldo Leopold, taught me to use willow like aspirin, kept me outside on a horse for fifteen hours every day. But Pop sprinkled his distrust of government on everything he taught me as a child, like salt on every meal. It felt like critical thinking for most of my life, but I realize now it was just seeing everything that one way.

I PREFER CAMPING WHEN the full moon brightens the midnight world into something warmer, more welcoming. The starlight seems brighter at full moon, even though I know that's not how light works. New-moon light is thin, muted, the distant shrill coyote yipping amplified, every crack of sagebrush an invisible threat. Even the temperature, which can be recorded objectively, felt colder than it should. I wasn't a quarter mile from the campsite Pop and I used every year, but I was on the adjacent BLM land. It's the same runoff stream I was camping next to, the same species of willow along its bank, but the patterns of the limbs, the music they made in the breeze—it was all off, somehow discordant. This landscape should feel familiar, safe, but at new moon it didn't quite.

I only knew I slept because I woke up disoriented and confused around 4 a.m. The inside of my tent was crusted with a layer of frost that sparkled a bit when my headlamp caught it at the right angle. It took a minute before I remembered that I was not a girl-child camping with her pop on land they owned free and clear to count the mating Gunnison sage grouse, but a grown-up lady scientist sneaking alone onto land she sold to pay her pop's medical bills.

If Pop dies, I won't go back to the Farallones. I will be the only one who cares about this lek, and these Gunnison sage grouse will be the only ones who really know me. I study endangered species that love their land so much they'll die without it, and I feel all the same emotions of twelve-year-old me, but lonelier somehow. I'm watching something beautiful pass away, the weight of the inevitable end heavy on my shoulders, and I know my best efforts to save them will never be enough, but I know now that I will stay and try, always and forever.

I was wiggling into my coveralls, which are warm but difficult to maneuver, when I heard the truck on the fire road. I turned off my lamp and grabbed Pop's old field binoculars. It was still dark. I couldn't see much, but I recognized Henson's old Ford. That truck has seen better days. It whines like it needs power steering fluid, and there's a quiet, rhythmic tick in the motor. It has a stocked shotgun rack inside the cab. That truck has all the wrong kind of noise, noise that could disrupt the lek, keep the birds from doing their mating dance.

I followed the runoff stream as I moved steadily closer to the truck, crouching low under cover of the willows along the bank. Nature might seem all peace and quiet, but she's deceptive that way, and I was thankful for how loud she really is. The noise of the stream covered the noise of my breath, my footsteps. I wanted to take pictures but didn't want to risk the glow of my phone. Henson was leaning against the truck bed, looking up at the stars. When he poured his coffee into the lid of his thermos, I was close enough to smell it. There were fuel cans in the back, shovels and rakes. It takes balls to burn public land, but plenty of ranchers have done it, claiming later that the fires on their own land just went a few acres wild. The one thing those birds need is abundant sagebrush, and getting rid of sagebrush is the whole point of a rancher burn in sage-steppe habitat. The fire makes room for cattle forage by erasing everything else.

"Hey girl," Henson said, and my body panicked, blood on fire. I thought to run, but he wasn't talking to me. He had a little girl with him, probably kindergarten age, wispy pigtails curling around her ears. Her coveralls were patched and worn, all her movements muted by the quilted fabric. She grabbed Henson's hand, and I wondered if she had the same egg-delicate eyes as her father.

"Can you carry this shovel?" Henson asked her, half whispering.

"I can see your breath, Daddy," the girl said. "It's steamy, like your coffee."

Henson smiled, and I did too. The girl threw her arms around his neck. I felt my heart fluttering again, my pulses warming. The sky lightened with the approaching dawn.

"Next time I come we should bring the horses," she said.

"Whatever you want, sweetheart." The two of them crossed to the other side of the truck, walked some distance away from it. Henson was stepping off an area, measuring it. The child was laboring at cartwheels, trying hard to work her limbs against the confines of her coveralls.

When Henson turned his back to the truck, I pulled the fuel cans and started dumping them into the dirt behind the back tires. The diesel fumes made the ground shimmer and shake, go blurry, filled up my nose so much that I thought no clean air would ever get in again. I couldn't take the ranch back from Henson, but he couldn't burn anything down without diesel. I heard a shout that might have been my name and dropped the cans. I snapped a picture for evidence and got out of there as fast as I could, tracking my way along the runoff stream deep into the BLM land. When the fumes cleared my head, I came back to myself. I tried to turn a cartwheel, but my center of gravity was all wrong.

BY THE TIME I got home the sun had cleared the range, burned the frost off the two-by-four railings. I spent the better part of last month building ramps, one out the back door of the house and one off the covered porch in the front. It's important to me that Pop can get in or out any door, not just for safety now that he's stuck in the damn wheelchair most of the time, but for dignity's sake. I'm no carpenter, but when you have YouTube and a garage full of tools you can teach yourself to build just about anything.

I squatted low to mount the binoculars back onto the rickety tripod I keep on the porch. The whole setup is asking for breakage and disaster, but birding is the only thing that has kept me sane in this house. I heard Pop roll over the threshold, felt the porch floor shudder just a little under the weight of his chair.

"Vera," he said. He put his hand between my shoulder blades. The warmth radiated down through my heart, my belly, my heels. I imagined it vining like roots down through the porch slats, breaking up the hardpan ground below.

I stayed frozen in place, kept Pop's hand on my back. I'd been short with Pop since I talked to Henson. I knew it. Now, I wanted to ask him whether I should take my pictures down to the BLM office, press for charges about the fences, the possible burn. I wanted to know where Pop's loyalty was, which side of his heart was bigger. I wanted to see how he'd react if I said, out loud, *Henson's cutting fence. He's going to graze the BLM and our lek. I could turn him in if I wanted to. He has the most precious little girl.*

I turned toward him, kneeling next to his chair. "There are only fifteen of our birds left," I said. I don't cry much, but I was crying then. "You wrote it down yourself, in your ledger. Why didn't you tell me?"

"Umm," Pop's brow furrowed. His hand moved toward his brow, but I caught it in both of mine, bringing it to the wet of my cheek. He shook his head sadly. "Dammit."

Pop can still swear like nobody's business. He can also sing every word to "Along Came Jones" by the Coasters and a number of other novelty tunes from his high school years. He sounds like the Swedish Chef from *The Muppet Show*, but he gets all the words. Julie tells me this is normal too, that profanity and music endure beyond prepositions and names, which feels like it must be an important fact about humans even though I can't exactly say how. It is very endearing and I marvel, with every crystal-clear Pop cuss, how much we don't know about the world of our own brains.

"Vera," Pop said, his tone serious. "Oreos."

I don't know what to worry about most, what to cling tightly onto and what to let go. Will too many Oreos give Pop a heart attack? Will Henson burn the lek? Will his beautiful pigtailed daughter find a way to love both the damn birds and the damn cows? There, on the porch, I wanted Pop to help me. I wanted him to teach me, better this time, how to untangle emotion from carefully recorded facts, how to reconcile the things I feel when they aren't the same, exactly, as the things I believe.

But instead, I said, "How many?"

He lifted his index finger and drew numbers in the air in front of his face, but I didn't catch them. Finally, he said, "Fifteen," then "No!" but I was already laughing, tears streaming down my face.

"Me too," I said. "Let's have fifteen." I wiped my nose with my sleeve. I felt greedy, ravenous. I wanted the most of everything.

"No. Ummm," Pop held up four fingers and said, "Two. No! Son of a bitch!"

"I'll just bring the whole bag," I said.

Pop can have as many Oreos as he wants.

IN 2005, SCIENTISTS BELIEVED they had confirmed an ivory-billed woodpecker, a single male, alive in the woods of Arkansas. Reports by amateur birders had been rejected for years by ornithologists, who insisted that ivory-bills were extinct, that the birders, lacking appropriate training, were simply encountering the luckier and still-in-the-world pileated woodpecker, an ivory-billed look-alike, and projecting (as humans do) their desire to see something both rare and lovely, declaring it ivory-billed. There are still, now, both believers and doubters. This, too, I'm supposed to read as a sign of hope, but again, I don't see it that way. I know exactly how lonely that poor bird must be, small in the world, the only one of its kind.

Alto Cumulus Standing Lenticulars

—

RUTH KNEW SHE WAS pregnant, but they'd driven the hundred miles from Gabbs to Tonopah anyway, for confirmation, she guessed, or for the change of scenery—though everywhere she looked there was desert and mountains, more desert, more mountains. At any rate, she was enjoying the small luxuries of the doctor's office—the glossy pages of a *Good Housekeeping* in the waiting room, a chalky mint from the reception counter bowl, a vinyl-cushioned chair that expelled air.

"Congratulations," the doctor said. "Looks like late February, early March for this one."

"Number four." This from Del, her husband, who scratched at his ear, grinning. "Great news."

Ruth couldn't pin the news to one side or another with any honesty at all. She'd been nineteen when she'd climbed into Del's old Falcon, left Colorado for glamorous nights in Vegas, stylish

dresses she didn't have to make herself, sets of matching jewelry—
but the only thing she'd accumulated since was children. Nothing
made Ruth appreciate the existing simplicities of her life like the
impending arrival of a new baby, lovable and helpless and full of
need, spiraling everything into chaos.

"Spring baby," Del said, grabbing her hand. "Brand-new when
the world is."

Ruth thought of her other children. Charley, eight years old,
sensitive, was prone to tantrums and odd rotating fascinations—
cloud formations by day, constellations at night, and now, because
it was October, migrating tarantulas. The girls, Nancy and Brenda,
seven and six, were all whisper and giggle, the bounce of their pigtails tapping gently, relentlessly, against their delicate shoulders.
She loved her kids, but she'd been working to stop at three.

Outside the office, Ruth squinted against the desert sun glare.
She considered the dusky greens and deep blues of the mountains
outside Tonopah—Mount Butler, Mount Oddie—the subtle com-
plexity of what had seemed, at first, a toasted desert monotone. A
few errant cumulus clouds had formed over the mountains, and
Ruth, despite her doubts, searched the sky for signs. Catholic school
had taught her to imagine the saints sitting on clouds with the well-
meaning ghosts of her dead ancestors, watching over her life, offering protection, guidance, intercession. It was both comforting and
disconcerting. She wanted to believe in it more than she actually did.

It was hard to accept that the world she'd left—her sisters whispering in her ears, her mother knitting her sweaters—was better
than the one she'd run to. She'd been taught all her life that her
future was sure to be brighter than her past. But yesterday's future
had turned into a vaguely bleak present, which made the past seem
especially shiny. In Ruth's daydreams, Colorado was just as she
left it. Amber-colored goblets arranged in her mother's kitchen

built-ins. An orderly line of three girlish peacoats draped over the mudroom's Shaker pegs. Coffee and Irish cream swirling in milk-glass mugs. In her daydreams, Ruth cooled her bare feet in the South Platte River.

"I've got to call home," she said. "Let Teresa know." Teresa, one year older than Ruth, had gone off to marry God the same year Ruth left with Del. She moved to the convent, changed her name to Sister Agnes Mary. Ruth saw Teresa as she had been, flirting with the boys at her sweet sixteen party, her green dress swirling around her shins, her hair in pin curls, lips stained punch-red with Kool-Aid and 7Up. Ruth had trouble remembering to call Teresa "Sister," could not conjure this new woman she had never met face-to-face. Only when she remembered the way Teresa had turned her appraising eyes toward Del, all those years ago, the way her head had bent under the weight of her disappointment, could Ruth picture Teresa in the gray habit and veil of their childhood teacher nuns. "That one's no good," Teresa had said. "So of course that's the one you want." Teresa, like the nuns Ruth had grown up with, was a confusing blend of compassionate love and harsh judgment. *Sisterly*, Ruth thought, embarrassed to be smiling at her own silent joke.

"I'll wait here," Del said. "Have a beer or two."

Ruth believed the nausea she felt then was as much homesickness as it was morning sickness, some result, certainly, of the difference between what she had and what she wanted.

Ruth dawdled. She bent down to pet a stranger's dog. She ran her fingers over the glass of the drugstore window. She picked up a piece of litter that turned out to be a crumpled brochure for the nursing program at the community college, smoothed it, considered it, put it in her pocket. Ruth had always wanted to be a nurse. After the blood and breath of birthing three babies, tending their fevers, bandaging minor wounds, she felt half a nurse already. She watched a lone tarantula pick a delicate path across the asphalt. She took deep breaths, counted the seconds between her steps.

IT TOOK A MOMENT for the women of the order to find the right nun, but finally Sister was on the line. "Everything okay, Ruth? The kids?"

Ruth closed her eyes. "Everyone's fine. It's me. I'm pregnant."

Sister made a joyful noise and Ruth settled. She could count on Sister to love her babies just as much as she did. "Congratulations," Sister said. "Ruthie, another baby! What blessings!"

The line crackled and popped. Ruth pressed her fingertips against the phone booth wall, felt the heat from the desert sun in the glass.

"I want this one to be born in Colorado," Ruth said, "but I still can't afford to get there." Ruth saved cash in an empty creamed corn can in the back of the pantry, that $3.72 the only secret she had in the world.

"The creamed corn can is low?" Sister's laugh was bright, cutting, like she knew something Ruth didn't. "I wish I could help you bring those babies home, Ruth, I do. But you know, vows of poverty. And Mom and Mano are barely getting by as it is."

Ruth knew what Sister wasn't saying out loud. *You made all the decisions that led to this.* "I wasn't asking for help."

"Weren't you?"

Someone Ruth didn't know was waiting outside the phone booth.

"I'd like to get a job, save my own money, but Del's not thrilled with the idea."

Del had, over the years of their marriage, lost a string of jobs dealing cards at cut-rate Vegas casinos. Not the big names, where he could have made a real living after Paul Anka or Tom Jones shows, but the trashier ones, daylight hours, penny-slot locals feeling flush on payday, a few low-stakes poker hands. Mining would be different, he'd told her, just before he moved the family from Vegas to Gabbs.

"It's 1970, Ruthie," Del had said, handing her a beer and then clinking his against it, as though she was as thrilled as he was. "New job for a new decade!"

"Plenty of mines in Colorado," she said. If they were going to leave Vegas, Ruth wanted all of Nevada in the rearview.

Del rolled his eyes, but still they sparkled. He pulled her close, tried to dance her across the kitchen. "You're missing the point, Ruthie. This is ground-floor luck. Magnesium is the mineral of the future!"

The stranger outside the phone booth looked impatient. "Does he have to know?" Sister asked. "About your job?"

Ruth tried to imagine a world in which she could have a secret job. It was ridiculous. Impossible. Sister didn't know anything about husbands. About kids. About the way a family was always around you and on top of you and inside you. About the ways it was possible to be surrounded and loved and crushingly lonely all at the same time.

"What do you mean does he have to know? Where would he think I was?"

"All right." Ruth heard Sister whisper to someone nearby, but she couldn't make out the words. "But if you found a job, you could tell him you got paid a little less than you did. Set a little by every week."

"You've got a lot of advice about how to lie," Ruth said, "for a nun."

"Would a creamed corn can full of money change Del's mind?"

Recently, Del had started telling stories about the incompetence of his direct supervisor and the generally dirty nature of work in the mine. It was a familiar pattern—complaints about the minutiae of the work, railing against workplace politics. Any day, he'd come home telling her he'd quit on some obscure principle, which would mean, of course, that he'd been canned.

"Might be." Ruth ran her hands up the metal of the cord, felt the joints bump against her fingertips. "Or maybe I'd just come home without him."

"I don't know, Ruth. You have to think of the kids."

Ruth sniffed. As if she ever stopped thinking about her kids, as if they weren't the first thing she always thought of, her closest, most essential thoughts. It was Del she didn't know how to think about. It wasn't indifference she felt, not really, it was more like having to decide whether she wanted to sink ever deeper into Del or whether she wanted him to disappear, or to disappear herself. These topics were not available to discuss with Sister. She couldn't possibly understand a marriage, but that wouldn't keep her from having strong opinions.

Sister kept going. "What I mean, Ruth, is that maybe there's some better use for that money, if you manage to save it, than just coming back to where you started."

Ruth pulled the nursing school brochure out of her pocket. *Good jobs helping others. Rural training initiative means flexibility for you.* She had never been jealous of Sister's vows, chastity least of all, but she'd been surprised by how green she'd felt when the church sent Teresa to college.

"I'll think on that one," Ruth said, and because she wanted to do that thinking before she talked any more to Sister about it, she asked, "How's Mano?"

Mano was their especially little sister, seventeen, the age difference between Ruth and Mano almost the same as the age difference between Mano and Charley.

"Flighty. Struggling to finish high school now that she knows she got her scholarship to that art school in Denver."

"She'll make it," Ruth said, picturing Mano flourishing her calligraphy pens.

"I'll make her."

Ruth could see Mano, dreamy, bent deeply into her art, Sister hovering behind her, checking the clock, encouraging strict production deadlines. Life in the church must be so simple, Ruth thought, if it allowed for such clarity, such a sense of control. "I have to go. There's a line for the phone."

"I miss you, Ruthie. Kiss those kids for me. Call soon."

Del was three sheets when she found him again, so she took the wheel of the Falcon. She wanted to pack the kids in the back and keep going all the way to Colorado, let her mother read them books, let Mano teach the girls to paint, let Sister explain the mystery of the Trinity to Charley. It wasn't Del's gathering restlessness she felt, it was her own. This time, Del couldn't "quit" fast enough.

The tires threw gravel as she pulled onto the road. "Jesus, Ruthie," Del said, "you don't have to donkey-stomp it."

A WEEK PASSED. RUTH was stirring the dinner beans when Charley stumbled into the kitchen of their trailer in Gabbs, pulling her toward the door. "Ma! Come outside! Come see!" Del looked up from the solitaire he'd spread across the gold Formica table, raised an eyebrow.

"Coming," she said. "Easy."

Outside, the Shoshone range had gone rosy, reflecting the pastels of the sky. The smell of sage was heavy, the dust baked stale. Her daughters were spinning, singing a song she didn't recognize.

"Do you see the clouds? Mom? Look up!" Charley was yelling. His voice was always louder than the moment demanded. It drew

unkind attention from others. A few neighbors stared from their
porches, a few darkened their windows. Not all of them went back
to minding their own business.

Ruth knelt down to be close to Charley's ear. She felt tense,
scrutinized. "You don't need to shout, Charley," she said. "I'm right
here."

The clouds were like giant discs lying on their sides, stacked in
twos and threes in the fading desert light—white tinged with gray,
the edges glowing in pinks and oranges.

Charley was still shouting. "Those are alto cumulus standing
lenticulars. They're made of gravity waves and wind." He threw his
arms around her neck. "Mom! Wind blows through them at hundreds of miles an hour, and they just stay there, hovering in place.
Like spaceships—people used to think they were spaceships." At
least half of Charley's fascination with the sky was the possible alien
life that could reside there. Del had encouraged this, his only real
point of connection with his son—Del was a scholar of alien abduction, a conspiracy connoisseur. Otherwise, Del seemed baffled by
Charley, perpetually annoyed.

Nancy rolled her eyes, whispered to Brenda, who giggled.

"Be nice, girls," Ruth said, but her daughters were only mir-
rors of the way the world seemed to react to Charley. It was a small
consolation that Charley himself did not register ridicule. Charley
radiated his enduring enthusiasm outward into the world despite
the world's cold reception.

Ruth flushed, felt saliva fill her mouth, just managed to turn
away before she vomited into the sagebrush.

Nancy rubbed her back, pulled a tendril of hair off the side of
her neck.

"Hey Charley," Brenda said, "let's play tarantula race."

Ruth watched her children get down on all fours and crawl,
frantically, toward the porch step finish line, then disappear inside

the house. When she could pull herself together, she followed them, the last heat of the day radiating up from the sand, warming her calves, her knees. She found a letter from Sister in the mailbox and waved it like a fan, cooling herself as she took one last look at Charley's clouds. She'd always thought they looked like stacked pancakes, those clouds, but as they drifted over the Shoshone peaks, it did seem likely that they were piloted, that they had a clear destination. Ruth was exhausted by the relentless efforts of piloting her own life, especially now that she had so many passengers.

Back in the kitchen, the kids swarmed around Del, who tried to explain the rules of solitaire.

"The goal is to get the suits in order," he said. "Line 'em right up."

The girls laughed and climbed into his lap. Charley nodded, stared reverently at the cards.

Sister had sent a small silver pendant engraved with a bearded man in robes, a staff in one hand, a giggling child on his shoulder. Ruth held it in her palm. The enclosed note read: *St. Christopher is the patron saint of travelers and children (also: gardeners, epileptics, and sufferers of toothache). Church lore says his protection is especially effective against lightning and pestilence. Keep him close, Ruthie.*

"Your sister," Del said, shaking his head, "is off her nut." He went back to his solitaire, humming "All-Around Man," and Ruth caught a glimpse of the carefree teenage Del she had loved once, for real. Her parents had chaperoned their first date to the movies. Del had put his coat over her lap to keep her warm. Underneath it, he'd rubbed his thumb back and forth against the inside of her thigh. It had been the most scandalous thing that had ever happened to her. She had wanted a whole life just like that.

Ruth tossed the envelope and laughed. "Sufferers of toothache," she said dismissively, but she spent some of her precious creamed corn dollars on a cheap chain from the pawnshop, wore

St. Christopher so that she could feel the silver against the bare skin over her heart, imagined the cells in her belly that would become her baby's fortified teeth.

RUTH WENT TO SEE about a job before she started to show, before the idea moved beyond impossible. The kids were off school, so she packed them into the Falcon, because what else was there to do with them?

Ranger Allen was a bear of a man, barrel-chested, with a beard and dark-rimmed glasses. He was about her age, sloppy. His park ranger's shirt was untucked, a grease stain above and to the right of where his navel would be. The scent of cigarettes actively vaporized out of his untrimmed, shaggy hair. The vaguely sour smell of the unwashed seeped from his clothes. Days, he was the ranger at Berlin-Ichthyosaur State Park, which contained both Berlin, a godforsaken ghost town from the Comstock Lode days, and the fossilized remains of the ichthyosaur, a prehistoric marine reptile that lived in the ocean that once covered the Great Basin. Nights, Allen hosted an AM radio show about alien sightings and cover-ups, ghost stories and government conspiracy. Del was Allen's most dedicated listener.

They found him working in Berlin, and she saw her children's eyes widen as they took the place in. There were a few splintered miners' shacks, a broke-down oxcart, an intricately carved wooden bureau. Someone had, optimistically, planted a scrawny young piñon among the cluster of long-abandoned homes. The Nevada sand swirled into spiraling clouds that rattled against the wooden walls, long since stripped of paint by the wild desert wind. Ruth could see at least five tarantulas migrating across the ghost town. She felt especially assaulted by spiders and the desert heat. Even in the cooling October afternoon, she couldn't keep herself from absorbing it. It left her feeling desiccated and spent, more raisin than grape. She did not want this place to get inside her. She was carrying enough already.

"Ruth," Allen said, nodding. He wasn't smiling, exactly. He looked bewildered.

"Hey Allen," she said. She pressed the nails of her fingers into both her palms. *Don't back down. Don't let him say no.* "I came to talk about the Help Wanted sign I saw over in town."

"That so?" Allen scratched at his beard. "It's custodial, mostly. Cleaning pit toilets. Picking up litter. It's not exciting."

Nancy and Brenda giggled, and she and Allen both turned toward the children. "I don't need more excitement," Ruth said.

Allen nodded. "Del know you're here?"

Ruth felt her heart seize. It was a truth-or-consequences moment, so she hedged. "Does it matter?"

Allen shrugged. "Not to me, I guess."

Charley had dropped in behind one of the tarantulas, whose movement seemed slower than the amount of motion it produced, a constant motion, all eight legs stretching and reaching at different times, the pattern incomprehensible, pipe-cleaner fuzzy. Charley took a step, stopped, waited a few beats of Ruth's heart, then stepped again. The tarantulas were the only thing that could bring Charley's attention down to earth. The girls followed close behind him, their skirts swishing softly against their legs.

"You like them spiders?" Allen asked Charley.

"They're tarantulas." Charley frowned as though he didn't want to talk about something Allen so clearly knew nothing about.

Be polite. Ruth wanted to correct him out loud but didn't. She didn't know what would be worse, in Allen's estimation, and she needed to make the right impression.

Allen bent down so he was eye level with the boy. "What else you know about?"

"I know twenty different constellations."

"Twenty?" Allen let out a low whistle. "That's a lot to know. You know Orion's Belt?"

"Of course," Charley rolled his eyes. "I could find Orion since I was three. Orion's boring."

Allen laughed. "I guess you aren't interested in the spaceships then. I thought you would be, being Del's boy and all."

"Spaceships?" Allen had Charley's attention. Ruth held her breath.

"They been here before, and when they came, they came right from Orion."

Allen stood up, turned his face into the blue sky, where Orion would be if it were dark. They searched the sky together for a minute, and when Charley turned back toward Ruth he was smiling— the same Charley smile, exponentially bright.

Brenda was letting a tarantula crawl on her arm. Ruth had not allowed this at first, but Charley had convinced her they were both unlikely to bite and not actually deadly poisonous. He'd looked it up in an ancient set of World Books in the school library.

"Are there ghosts here?" Nancy asked Allen.

Ruth watched Brenda's tarantula unfold its first set of legs, which stretched delicately forward and planted themselves, levered the crawling mass of the body forward. The creatures did not look at all efficient, Ruth thought, but they sure did cover country.

"There's nothing to be afraid of," Allen said. "Most days the population of Berlin is entirely tarantulas."

"Thomas Edison invented a machine that could call the dead," Charley shouted. Nancy winced, covered her ears. "Or he tried to. It didn't work."

"Thomas Edison invented the lightbulb, not a dead guy phone," Brenda said.

Ruth sighed. None of her children had made friends at school, but she didn't worry about the girls. She had shared not just a room but a bed with Sister when they were young, Mano joining them straight out of the crib. Ruth knew sister love was like a gas—it could lift the barometric pressure of the entire atmosphere if you needed it to.

"But if there are ghosts," Allen said, "they're over there in the old hospital. The doctor was nothing but a Chicago stockyard butcher. Could be the ghosts of his lost patients haunt this spot, only they must be scared of tarantulas, since I don't see any here now."

Brenda giggled, intertwined her fingers so that the tarantula could walk from one arm to the other. Nancy went wide-eyed, scooped a tarantula off the ground, held it between her body and the old hospital. Ruth clutched St. Christopher. Charley went back to tarantula-stalking, tracing their paths on a piece of lined binder paper. Sometimes he stopped and held the map he had created up to the sky, studying both intently.

"What are you looking for?" Allen asked.

"Patterns," Charley said. "Trajectory matches."

"Smart," Allen said. "You should try it at night too, against the stars."

Charley and Allen were like Sister, Ruth supposed, all of them seekers of faith, or magic, or whatever meaning could be found combining the two. Ruth dismissed the alien talk from the men in her life the same way she'd walked away from Catholicism, with just the tiniest nagging doubts that it all might, in fact, be true. Ruth imagined St. Christopher at the controls of a lenticular spaceship, heading for Orion's Belt. She imagined each star in the constellation a nosy ghost ancestor with strong opinions about her choices.

"What do you see?" she asked, kneeling down next to Charley.

"I haven't been looking long enough to know."

She could prove nothing, disprove nothing. She decided then to stop doubting Charley, to stop worrying about how he did or did not fit into the world. What if a hand-drawn map of tarantulas skittering across the desert really could unlock some mystic secret of the cosmos? Navigation might be the boy's hobby now, but Ruth recognized its potential for practical application.

"That's a smart kid," Allen said. "Can you start tomorrow?"

Ruth sent a small prayer of gratitude to St. Christopher then, for Allen's kindness to her boy, for the job she needed, that nobody, so far, was suffering toothache or other pestilence. Ruth's eyes followed her children's fragile limbs as they stretched and contracted into the landscape.

RUTH WAS AN UNLIKELY state parks employee. After a few months on the job, her pregnant belly stuck out so far she tore a small hole in her sweater's seam. Everything about her was poorly suited for the environment. The February wind blew steady and unpleasant, pinning the flared legs of her park uniform against her shins. She climbed into the cab of the truck for relief, pulled a stocking cap over her hair. Desert sand made its way through the knit of her wool socks.

Allen cracked the driver-side door. "Ruth? You okay in there?"

"Just wanted a break from the wind," she said. "I'm fine."

"You need me to call Del?"

"He's probably not home."

She had taken Sister's advice, lied to Del about her wages. She was adding to her creamed corn can every two weeks, praying to St. Christopher for the journey back home. Allen looked at her for a long time, shook his head, went back to work.

Ruth tried to bend down to remove her shoes, but the child in her womb moved in protest, pressing down on her bladder just enough for a small amount of urine to release, to leave a wet spot on her panties. She felt one of the child's limbs extend down farther than it should, passing what she felt must be the barrier between belly and leg. The pain was sharp. Ruth felt as though she was being peeled from the inside, as though the membranes holding her together would hang now, stripped and useless, from her muscle and bone. Ruth drew in a quick breath and held it, waiting, willing the pain to spread out from her pelvis and into her knees, to make her arms shake and weaken. She wanted the pain to be brief but all-encompassing, to have her body store the memory of it, to practice. This child would come anytime now, and she needed to prepare herself, to be ready for the familiar ways it would rip her apart.

The final chore of every workday required sweeping the pavilion that held the ichthyosaur fossils, dinosaur reptilians that swam well but had to surface to breathe. Ruth struggled to discern the fossil outline in the assortment of rocks and boulders in the display, even though she'd seen Allen's presentation for park visitors a million times, watched him map the skeleton by pointing to various areas on a small toy dolphin. She could not identify the creature's backbone, could not tell its skull from its feet, but she felt a deep ache of empathy for this poor animal, sunk for all eternity into the sand, everything cool and familiar having evaporated, the world dried-up, unrecognizable, tarantulas migrating annually over its bones.

"It's some kind of instinct," Ruth said. She hadn't seen a tarantula in months, but she thought about them all the time, pictured their fuzzy legs in perpetual motion. What was the chemistry driving their built-in sexual clocks? Did they, like Ruth, regret the distances love required?

"What kind?" Allen asked, but she didn't answer. Ruth put her hand on her belly. Her baby's hand pushed back against it, hard, like it needed her attention, like it had something important to tell her.

RUTH CAME HOME TO see Del sitting in a folding chair outside the trailer. His short-sleeved gray coveralls were unzipped above his belt so that Ruth could see a sunburn on a V-shaped strip of his pale chest. He hadn't gotten that underground.

"Something happen at work today?" she asked, but she already knew the answer.

"Things ain't gonna work out at the mine," Del said.

"So let's go home." She felt the baby squirming. Maybe now it could be born in Greeley, in the same hospital she and Del had been born in. Her mother would knit a hat. Mano would paint its portrait. Sister would coo at the wrinkled newborn, fill its ears with whispered blessings.

Del shrugged, pointed toward the mountains with his palms up, as if he was offering her some gift. "This is as good a home as any."

Del was so close that Ruth could feel the warmth of him on her shoulder. She stepped away, and they watched Charley, alone, head for the edges of the trailer park, back toward the scrub sage foothills of the Shoshones. Ruth felt sadness settle, again, all around her. There wasn't a single tree within walking distance for Charley and the girls to climb, no ancient catalpa with its June blossoms, no bean pods to throw at one another.

"I got a new job. Trucking company. They're picking me up tonight."

"Driving trucks?"

"Reno, first, then down to San Francisco tomorrow. From there, they say they got at least two weeks of routes. Long-haul."

Ruth sat back down in the chair. She kicked her shoes off with a strength she hadn't expected and her left shoe flew gracefully, almost with purpose, landing in the scrub sagebrush just past the area she had cleared as a front yard. Ruth thought she saw a tarantula skittering across the patch of light brown dirt that, having been liberated of its anchoring vegetation, puffed up around them, but in February, it seemed unlikely.

"You're going to leave us here and go off yourself?" she said. She felt unbearably heavy. She looked at her shoe in the sagebrush. She left it go. "To drive a truck?"

"Look in the want ads. There's no jobs but at the mine."

"But the kids, and the baby coming." Ruth's arms had gone dead. It would take a lot, she thought, to move her arms right now. The whole of her body felt defeated, all her energy sucked dry. And something else, something cool like the desert evening. Relief, maybe. And something even more, a longing for her own solitary long-haul route. Jealousy, certainly.

"Look, I'm not leaving you, Ruth. It's a job, is all. I'll send the paychecks."

Ruth dropped her chin and closed her eyes, and the relief of not seeing in that moment made her wish all her other senses could be so easily blocked, that she could make herself stop hearing, stop feeling through some series of actions as simple as blinking.

"Unless you got any better ideas," Del said.

Charley and the girls had returned from their wanderings, had gathered around the porch, straining to hear every word without being caught listening. Charley stood close to his sisters, as though he wanted to try to catch the bad news before it hit them, soften the delivery.

"Guess not," Ruth said. "Guess it sounds like this all works out real well for you. All that roaming, and then you drop in to see the family once every two weeks."

Del shook his head. "You'll get over it, Ruthie. You'll see. It's for the best."

"Not my best."

"I gotta pack," Del said, and he disappeared into the trailer.

"Daddy's leaving?" Nancy said, and when Ruth nodded, the girls sat down at her feet. Brenda leaned her head against Ruth's leg. Nancy kept her back straight. Too fragile for contact, she needed only proximity.

Charley took her hand, pointed it above the tallest peak of the Shoshones, the trailing shadow of the sunset drama spread in all directions. "Look, Ma," he said, wiping the tears off her cheek, "those are cirrus clouds, and they're all pink and purple. I think they're the happiest clouds, don't you? Birthday-streamer clouds." He stroked Ruth's cheek with the back of his hand. It was the most tender anyone had been with her for ages.

"Thanks, buddy," she said, finally, drawing him close to her in an awkward hug, stroking Nancy's hair with her fingers, feeling Brenda warm against her shin.

Babies weren't the only thing that could upend an entire world. The world changed fast or slow for a million reasons. There weren't always nine months of knowing what was coming. There wasn't always time to prepare.

AFTER A FEW DAYS, Ruth moved Del's empty chair away from the family table. She taught Charley how to keep the handles of the pot turned sideways to avoid spills and burns. She told her kids that after school was all-they-could-watch TV so long as they behaved, so long as they could fend for themselves. During the after-school hours, when she was at work, she imagined the trailer on fire, imagined tarantula bites, imagined poking Del's two eyes with her fingers when he next came by for a weekend. Evenings, she reread the nursing school brochure, as though she'd find new instructions printed there, not just what but *how* and *should*. She wished a dead ancestor would lean down from the heavens and tell her whether she was fooling herself.

Sometimes the kids came with her to work, spent their days in Allen's one-room trailer on the outskirts of Berlin. Every time they went, Charley tapped the handmade sign on Allen's door that read: *Ranger Station.* The trailer was full of machines and panels Ruth thought must be for radio broadcasting, for all of Allen's lonely, conspiracy-minded midnight transmissions.

"Del called in last night," Allen said, "with some theories about mind control."

Ruth rolled her eyes. "If he calls back," she said, "tell him to send the rent." Del didn't call her from his long-haul routes. Apparently, he prioritized the aliens.

Allen had been washing his clothes more often. Last week, he'd trimmed his beard. Ruth kept just enough distance to discourage him. She was, after all, still married.

"You getting by all right, Ruth?" Allen's brow furrowed. He looked worried, and Ruth felt compelled by the sorrow she saw behind it.

Ruth shrugged, nodded. Allen meant well, but beyond loyal friendship, beyond this job, what did he really have to offer?

A WEEK PASSED. RUTH was sweeping the fossil pavilion at the end of the day when she felt her belly contract and harden, felt the heat in her arms and legs drain inward, concentrate into the boulder her womb had become. She tried to lean on the broom, to stay upright, but couldn't manage it. She dropped into a squat and linked her elbows around the bends of her knees. She closed her eyes, blowing out hard, emptying all her air, waiting for this wave of pain to pass. The broom slapped the floor, the sharp initial sound softening into gentle echoes that intertwined with the rhythm of her panting. The effect was not unlike radio static. Her left hand gripped the ichthyosaur's fossilized eye socket.

"Allen," she said. It came out as a whisper. She grunted, trying to force her voice back into her throat, trying to muster a shout. She thought of her kids, at home in the trailer in Gabbs, felt relief they weren't with her. She staggered herself out of the pavilion, into the gathering dusk. "Allen!"

And then she was alone in the throes of another contraction. Her ears were full of the tidal rushings of her own blood, of her amniotic fluids, all her salty marine internals muting the outside world. She was inside her own head now, focused. The pain moved from her womb to her lower back. She felt the baby flip inside her. This she had not felt before, not with the others. She tried to morph her screams into a level, steady keening. She imagined her breath catching her pain, imagined the way both breath and pain would leave her, diffuse into the air around her, the way she would have to breathe them both back into herself.

She felt the baby turn again, and the pain moved back into her belly. Her pelvic muscles felt alive, as though each fiber was moving individually and at cross-purposes to the others, like a writhing pile of mating snakes. She was overwhelmed by her desire to bear down, to push into the earth's gravity. The baby would not wait for safety. Ruth wanted, more than anything, her sisters, but she wanted also, just a little bit, Del.

Ruth caught the sliver of new moon surrounded by wispy, long clouds. Ruth tried to name them. Cirrus? Cumulus? She couldn't pin them down, and if the angels were gossiping with her dead ancestors about her current predicament, she didn't want to know. The stars were coming in bright against the darkening skyline but seemed in motion, as if they were being drawn in real time by frantic Spirograph. Bad enough the other children had to be from Vegas. This baby would be from nowhere, a ghost-town baby, born on top of a fossil. She could not take back any of the decisions that had led her here. This is where she found herself, so this is where her baby would be born.

Allen came in then, stopped still with shock. He gagged, then bent forward as he sat down on a bench, his head in his hands.

"We have to get you to a hospital." He didn't look up. His concern was directed toward his boots.

"There's no time." Ruth wriggled out of her nylons and dropped into a squat. She rested her forehead against the beam of the fossil pavilion. The pressure was somehow soothing, and it allowed her to balance without using her hands.

She breathed into her body's gathering, bearing down in her womb, trying to maneuver her rib cage lower, pulling her neck downward until it felt there was nothing at all between her chest and her chin. She tried to relax. She'd done this three times already. If she were in the hospital, she'd have a nurse to coach her. Here in the desert, she'd have to be her own nurse. At the peak of the contraction she reached her right hand up and into herself, screaming her wild misery into the night but willing her hand to be gentle, gentle, as she pulled, lightly, lightly, down on her child's shoulder. The head cleared and the rest of the child dropped. Ruth held it with both hands, pushing her forehead into the beam so that she would not fall, would not lose her grip. Behind her, she heard a tremendous flopping thump.

The boy was blue, wrapped in his own umbilical. Ruth made short work of unwrapping it, of clearing the clotted white mucus from the baby's nose and mouth. She turned to ask Allen for his ranger's shirt, for anything to wrap the child in, but Allen was still crumpled in a full faint. She took off her own state park sweater, wrapped her baby tight against the chill. When she heard his indignant, hungry cries, she put her back against the beam and started crying herself, shivering on the cool desert ground. The baby rooted

against her belly as she waited to deliver the placenta. Beyond his
newborn head, she could see the full glory of Orion's Belt. Something in the center of the constellation was flashing on and off, or
maybe it was distant lightning from a threatening storm, or it was
just the way she saw everything differently through her tears.

She wanted to call Sister. *I'm naming this one after St. Christopher*,
she'd say. *Because I miss you. And to protect him from lightning.*

Charley would be taking charge of things in the trailer, she
thought, calming the missing-mother panic of his sisters with tales
of constellation aliens, spaceship abductions, and lenticular pancakes. Her sweet, awkward firstborn forever scanning the sky for
signs of life and omens, trying to show everyone around him all the
potential it contained, to teach them to see what he saw. Baby Chris
was squalling now with healthy lungs, the tiny fingers of one hand
wrapped tightly around her index finger, his other hand stretched
out, pointing toward the ichthyosaur. She turned his head toward
the window so that he, too, could look toward the stars.

"Someday, you'll see how bright they are," she whispered.

It was possible, Ruth thought, that being from nowhere might
somehow allow this baby to belong everywhere, to call anywhere
home.

Allen crawled beside her. He reached toward the baby, but then
pulled his hand away. "We're going to have to get you a raise."

Ruth laughed, shivered, tightened her arms around the bundle
of baby on her chest. "I'll take it."

THE FOLLOWING WEEK, RUTH rocked a sleeping Chris on the
porch while the other three slept inside. She worried St. Christopher between her thumb and forefinger. She had one blanket over
her shoulders and one on her lap. The night air was headed toward
frost. It still carried the fragrant sage scent, but the dusty tones

had shifted to something deeper, prehistoric. Del had come home for just two days to meet his new son, dance the girls around the kitchen, give Charley a UFO-shaped key chain.

As Del drove away, his return unspecified, Ruth realized she didn't miss Del so much as she missed his hands—hands that could button a child's coat, fix a dinner, warm her shoulders with their warmth and their weight. Any man had hands. Allen had hands, but they came with strings attached, and she wanted the strings less than she wanted the hands. Ruth had saved enough to get in the Falcon and drive, job be damned and Del, back to Colorado, but she hadn't left Gabbs. The Falcon's tires were threadbare but roadworthy, and Ruth had decided to drive them toward her first nursing class instead of retreating back home. The creamed corn money added up either way.

That night, when she waddled into the kitchen to count it, the creamed corn can was gone. Ruth felt everything in the hot center of herself twisting—gut, throat, heart. She reached for the countertop, heaving her weight just in time, and vomited into the chipped porcelain sink. She imagined Del in Vegas, turning her creamed corn money into slot tokens and lost potential. She imagined him in a liquor store, turning her creamed corn money into a happy solo buzz.

What now, St. Christopher?

The silence was infuriating. She needed spiritual guidance that had some volume. She checked on her children, their sleeping bodies illuminated by moonlight, and then she swaddled Chris tight and drove down to the pay phone.

The phone rang and rang until she heard a drowsy greeting, then whispered feminine commotion, and then, finally, Sister.

"Ruth?" Sister said. "It's the middle of the night here."

"Same here."

"You woke everyone up."

"It's not fourth grade. You can't rap my knuckles with a ruler."

"Ruthie," Sister said, "you sound crazy."

Ruth tried to picture what nuns wore to bed, what Sister looked like in this moment. She imagined multiple layers of garments, complicated hook-and-eye fastenings.

"Can I still pray to St. Christopher if I'm stuck here in Gabbs?"

"Prayers are like the radio, Ruthie. You never know who's listening exactly, but someone always is." There was a pause. "Can you please tell me what's happening?"

"Del stole my creamed corn money."

"Del," Sister said, expelling his name with her breath, almost grunting him out. Chris startled, blinked his drowsy newborn eyes, settled back into sleep. "I'm sorry, Ruth."

Ruth slumped down onto the sidewalk under the pay phone, her back against the cinder-block wall, the desert sky stretching endless in front of her, her newborn son cradled in one arm. She felt comfortable with the immensity of the sky. She hoped Charley was right about the aliens, that Del and Allen knew more than it seemed possible they could. The more life there was, the less lonely any one person had to feel, the more hope for a connection.

"What do you think you'll do now?" Sister had turned her volume down, or there was something wrong with the line. It was hard to hear.

"I'll just have to start over." She wasn't ready, yet, to tell Sister about the nursing school. At least it was a safer place to put the money than a creamed corn can, even if it was a longer road back to Colorado. A way to believe, again, in her own glittering future. Something, like her children, that she'd have for herself.

Chris stirred in her arms. Ruth thought about her girls' giggled secrets, about Charley's hand on her cheek. She watched the moon traverse the patterned stars, wondered which constellations Charley would map for her if he was awake, which individual shining points of light, grouped together, would make a whole story.

Early Warning Systems

—

IN MARCH OF 1986, Mano Reichert climbed onto the roof of her childhood home in an effort to see Halley's Comet. Though the comet was supposed to be brighter from the southern hemisphere, Mano had a set of binoculars and a positive outlook. She'd been stargazing from the roof of her house since she was ten years old, the same year her then teenage sisters, Teresa and Ruth, left home within months of each other. For Mano, their especially little sister, suddenly alone, lonely, bereft, the roof was a tiny rebellion. Her parents, who loved her best when she entertained herself, were rarely curious about her location, and her sisters, who would certainly have told her it was too dangerous, had taken their opinions and their protection with them when they left.

Mano had always struggled to see the constellations by tracking stars. Instead, she could focus on the negative space and find the silhouettes that were outlined in the sky, the light of the stars a bright outline of inky blue-black beauty—her sisters in profile, the trailing seed pods of a catalpa tree, a crisscrossed map of the interstate highway system. She knew the sky shifted with the earth's orbit and rotation, but slowly, nearly imperceptibly. Mano loved anything—airplanes, satellites, comets—that flashed fast and bright across her familiar skies, helped her see them differently. In art school, Mano had learned that vision was a layered thing, something beyond physical sight. Vision required clarity. You could paint the world exactly as you saw it, but without a coherent sense of context, without intentional meaning-making, you wouldn't end up with art. For years, Mano had made half a living painting portraiture and landscapes for tourists outside Rocky Mountain National Park, an application of her talent from which she had been unable to make any meaning at all.

"I heard it's years of luck if we see it." Ruth, Mano's oldest sister, joined her on the roof as often as she could these days. Ruth worked the night shift as a labor and delivery nurse, and when she wasn't working, she slept, her snores as rhythmic and patterned as a washing machine cycle. Ruth's enthusiasm for stargazing hinted that the romantic Ruth, the wild teenage dreamer Mano had idolized as a girl, still lived somewhere underneath the increasingly harsh practicality of Ruth's middle-aged-working-single-mother-of-four persona. "Once-in-a-lifetime sighting, once-in-a-lifetime luck."

"Once in your lifetime, maybe," Mano countered. She was thirty-three years old, nine years younger than Ruth, had every intention of living the seventy-five years it would take to see the comet again in 2061. When she saw Ruth start to argue, Mano cut her off. "You don't know how the world will change any more than I do. Maybe we'll all live longer than we think." She said this more to argue than because she believed it. Mano kept up with the news, read her horoscopes. When examined with any honesty, all future indicators were bleak. And then there were the dead fish. Mano made the other half of her living manning the reception desk at the city of Loveland's water treatment facility. Two days before, there

had been a massive fish kill in the river, and while it was still officially an unsolved mystery, Mano was pretty sure that Keith, her
boss, and Lloyd, his boss, knew something she didn't.

Ruth pursed her lips and looked back up at the sky. Mano felt
the roof solid underneath her. The house was well built, sturdy, and
the family shifted in and out of its shelter as needed. Their father had
passed years ago, and then their mother. After that, Ruth and her
four kids had come back to Colorado, moved in with Mano. Teresa,
who had become Sister Agnes Mary, who lived now in the church
annex downtown, who taught kindergarten at St. Paul's, stopped by
when she could for coffee, for a few hands of rummy. Three of Ruth's
four kids had grown and flown since then; the last, Chris, sixteen,
emerged from the basement only occasionally, for snacks. Mano had
moved out too, after her wedding the previous summer.

"I saw Rick in line for confession earlier," Ruth said, "but I
didn't see you. I thought he'd come with you tonight." Ruth looked
away from the sky to stare at Mano. Behind her, Mano saw a new
silhouette—a trout curving mid-glide. She wondered what, exactly,
Rick had confessed.

Mano had knelt with Rick in front of the altar at St. Paul's
Catholic Church, had made a number of promises she had, at that
time, fully planned to keep. Rick, also, had seemed sincere. Rick
was even more obsessed with Stevie Nicks than she was, and in
those early summer months of their marriage he'd loved to watch
Mano undress to the early version of "Sorcerer" from his 1974
Buckingham-Nicks demo. Mano would move like the white-winged
dove, building intensity with the music, and always, after, Rick lay
on his belly, turned his face toward hers, draped his arm across
the soft skin of her chest as they both drifted into sleep. But the
marriage had flashed hot, cooled quickly. Mano knew she was no
longer the only woman lying naked with Rick, smoking cigarettes,
listening to "Wild Heart."

Mano wondered if Ruth knew too, if that's why she was asking. She had a way of knowing things she'd never been told directly.

Rick had backed out of comet-viewing at the last minute. "Your sister makes me nervous," he'd said. "And besides, I'm close to something in this game. I'm sure of it."

Rick had spent a month's salary on an Apple IIe computer, become obsessed with a video game called Cranston Manor. From what Mano could tell, it was post-apocalyptic, the player looting a mansion that had been hastily and mysteriously abandoned. Details were scarce, so she invented scenarios—acid rain aerosoling into atmosphere, nuclear winter, or maybe the cyanide gas in the comet's tail was potent enough, as people used to believe, to decimate humanity. The game involved endless wandering through pixilated parlors and drawing rooms and garden labyrinths for items of dubious value the player could collect. The program would tell Rick, in text under the picture, things like: *You are in the library. There is some moldy cheese here*, and Rick would type, *Get cheese*. And then later the program would say: *You are in the smoking room*, and he would type, *Drop cheese*, just to see what would happen.

Rick had, one time, tried to teach her how to play. Mano collected items as advised: *Get dagger. Get crystal. Get bottle full of diamonds*. She suspected that she would eventually have to fight the mysterious suit of armor that appeared, ghost-like, in various rooms, but she lost interest before she discovered any possible use for the things she carried. Not the dagger. Not the bottle full of diamonds. Not even the game itself made her feel any closer to Rick, all her familiar loneliness back in the atmosphere, as toxic as anything else.

Back on the roof, Ruth pointed at a spot in the sky. "Is that it? Can you see it?"

"Shhhhh." Mano gazed through her binoculars. She thought she saw the comet, not like a star, no visible tail, just a hazy spot of sky gone a bit lighter than the rest. *That figures.* She'd have to believe she'd seen the comet the same way she believed Rick was home alone playing a video game, by just deciding it was true, by not thinking too hard about it.

"Don't shush me, Mano. We're not bird-watching. Talking isn't going to scare the comet away." Ruth took the binoculars. "Not much to look at, is it?"

Mano tried to focus on the spot where the comet was, though she wasn't sure she could see it with her naked eyes. Mano was surprised at the desperation she felt, how much she'd been hoping to see the comet clearly. She'd been trained to see both shadow and light. She wanted the comet to send some sort of signal. *I could at least use some luck*, she thought. *Get comet*, she thought.

THE NEXT MORNING, WHEN she arrived at work, there was a jelly roll and a Styrofoam cup of black coffee on her desk, steam rising from the opening in the plastic lid. A gift. Keith. She could hear him talking on the phone in his adjacent office. Mano's job at the water treatment plant was easy and relentlessly boring—most days she wondered why they kept a receptionist at all. The water treatment facility was spared the public wrath of, say, the utilities department, where citizens regularly marched themselves down in person to shout about their bills. Nobody came to the water treatment office. People rarely called. She sipped the coffee while watching a few trout glide behind the glass of the tank that took up half the wall opposite her desk. Trout did better in the river's upper sections, where the water was colder, but they could be found in the river down here as well, and Lloyd insisted on having a few in the office tank. Recently, the city had cut the budget for the tank service contractor, and she and Keith had both been pretending they didn't notice how filthy things were getting in there.

One way Mano passed the time was to spend hours, on-the-clock, with her oil pastels, working to capture the rosy blush of trout gills, the way the red stripe along the side of the greenbacks faded in and out, almost woven through the deep green-brown skin, the way the rainbows kept a consistent blush that practically glowed. She'd named every rainbow trout in the tank Stevie Nicks, while the greenback cutthroats were all Lindsey Buckinghams. The tank, full of river water, was meant to display the health of the ecosystem, but it also served as an early warning. If something was killing fish in the river, it killed the fish in the tank, too.

When Mano finished her coffee, she wiped the jelly donut out of the corners of her mouth and opened the door to Keith's office, already unbuttoning her shirt. The pastels had led to the other way Mano passed the time at work, which was by fooling around with Keith. Keith disapproved of naming river trout, but he'd insisted on hanging her paintings all over the office. Mano wished she was as enthusiastic about the work as he was. She'd tried to capture their personalities, the essential beauty in their laconic gliding, but all she'd managed were trout—technically perfect, realistic, lifeless. All sight. No vision.

"They're beautiful," Keith had said, blushing, looking at her, not the pastels, and Mano had been both touched by his awkward proposition and embarrassed by his innocent sincerity.

"Morning," she said. Keith usually smiled with his mouth closed, self-conscious, she assumed, about the gaps in his teeth. It was endearing when he forgot himself and really let a smile rip, his teeth adorable for all their imperfections. She smiled back as she shook herself out of her blouse.

Keith started to undo his belt. It was only ever the two of them in the office, but the possibility that someone might show up and surprise them in the act made it all the more delicious. "You see the paper today? Someone wrote in saying it was the comet that killed all those fish."

Mano's mind went spastic, gummed up, *What kind of theory is that?* She'd read that when the comet went through in 1901, people stocked up on "comet pills" from quack doctors. They'd taken them as an antidote to poison and ended up poisoning themselves. She hadn't expected similar nonsense in 1986, but there it was, in the newspaper, more comet conspiracy.

And then Keith was kissing her and she let herself sink into the distraction of him without asking any of the thousand follow-up questions that occurred. She'd come to the job in September a happy newlywed, but by New Year's, she'd started smelling perfume she didn't wear and sex she hadn't had all over Rick. Mano wanted to believe that Keith was her way of moving carefree and easy through the rich banquet of life, same as Rick, sampling its delights at will, but she knew at least part of what she saw in Keith was the chance for petty revenge. And why not? She'd been raised to believe that marriage would mean she'd never have to feel lonely again. When the lonely came back, prickly, cutting, an infestation, it had been easy to accept Keith's invitations. She'd come to crave his attention, his affection, the same way she craved sunbathing—it felt so good she overdid it, every time, and wound up burnt-red with all her regrets.

The business between them lasted ten, fifteen minutes, and when she came back out to the reception desk, every last fish in the tank was dead. Again.

"Why is this happening?" She half yelled this, which summoned Keith, who walked into the reception area with his pants still undone, tucking in his shirt.

Keith peered into the tank, as if getting closer to the algae smeared glass would make it easier to see through. "I gotta call

Lloyd." Lloyd was the big boss, the director of Water and Power. When he'd shown up to the first fish kill, Lloyd had blustered around for a while before he and Keith had talked in hushed tones. It was clear there was something they didn't want her or anyone else, probably, to know.

"You sure?" Mano asked. Lloyd was a real hothead, prone to shouting, quick to assign blame. It was bound to be a trial, getting Lloyd involved.

Keith zipped his pants. "We can't have people drinking this. We have to get off the river and run the reservoir instead. And anytime I switch the intakes I have to tell Lloyd."

Two Lindsey Buckinghams were floating, their sides exposed so that it was easy to see, from the top of the tank, the way the spot patterns were sparse around their faces, the denser clusters near their tail fins, as though a magnet had pulled the spots from one end of the fish to the other. A couple of Stevies had sunk to the rocks at the bottom of the tank, the pink-blush stripe of their sides muted through the dirty glass. Mano pressed both her hands into her chest to hold her sinking heart steady. Tears wet her eyelashes and she blinked them back. She would do a lot of things at work, but she knew better than to cry.

"Lloyd is going to hand me my ass over this," Keith said, "and I'm the one who told those guys they had to clean up their act."

Mano thought to make a joke about his hands and her ass, but it didn't seem like the time. "What guys? Who would do this?"

Keith picked up the phone receiver and started dialing. Mano pressed the button on the saddle to cut the line. "Keith. Tell me."

Keith looked at the ceiling, as though he'd find the right way to live printed in bold on the asbestos tiles. "Okay, but you have to keep it quiet, all right? It's the construction on the road upstream. Those guys have a reputation for being sloppy with chemicals, and they don't seem too fussed about a few dead fish."

Mano worked to integrate this new horror into the story. She spread all ten fingers against the glass of the tank and pressed until the pads went pale. The rainbow trout were her favorites, Stevie over Lindsey forever. But the greenback cutthroat had been declared extinct in the 1930s, and who didn't love an underdog? Since they'd found some alive back in the fifties, the Fish and Wildlife Service had been breeding them in fisheries, stocking the rivers, hoping they'd take, once again, to their native habitat. To see them floating there on the top of the giant tank, just under the sign *Big T. River*, made her more angry than she could remember ever being. How many fish had to die before someone stopped this?

Keith's panic was seeping into the office air. Lloyd was yelling through the receiver like an angry teacher out of a Charlie Brown cartoon.

"Okay," Keith said. "Yeah." He covered the bottom end of the receiver with one hand and waved his other hand erratically. She thought he was swatting at a fly until she realized he was beckoning her. Mano pretended she didn't understand, because there was nothing in it for her. She held up one finger as though she would be right back, and fled outside, squinting against the spring sunshine.

Tiny nuthatches crawled sideways, upside down, at all angles in their quest to pull sustenance from the cottonwood bark, their frantic group yammering markedly less adorable than their appearance. The riverbank was lined with dead fish, dozens of them, the water undulating their corpses in tiny rhythmic waves. Twice now. Mass death—trout, human—was too much to bear. Unless the face of one dear and beloved individual stared lifeless from the void, it was easy to keep the surrounding bodies anonymous, to forget they were each of them once alive, maybe beloved. Most humans did not love trout the way Mano did, which made it especially easy for them to look away, deflect blame onto the comet.

A breeze rattled through the cottonwoods, sent gray-yellow

leaves left over from autumn scratching across the single-track trail and into the newly green tufts of buffalo grass that signaled spring-time. Mano took out her sketchbook, started in with a pencil, dead trout on dead trout on dead trout, just as they appeared from the riverbank, dead trout clogging every stagnant section of river, her heart flooding and clogging and swelling until the pressure was too much. She put the pencil away and closed her eyes. It was painful to look closely enough at the world to draw it. It made her itch. It made her ache.

The mid-river current sent flashes of reflected sun, too bright to bear. Mano tried to read the flashing as code, but she couldn't find any discernible pattern. She found an empty Pepsi bottle someone had dumped along the bank. She knelt down in the damp sand and used a stick to push the fish corpses out into the current. She filled the bottle with river water, watched the bodies of the fish swirl in a lazy downstream eddy. *Get evidence.*

Mano held the bottle close to her face, watched as particulates swirled, lazy and lovely, through the cloudy mirk. She didn't have any clear intentions just then for the water or the sketch, but she thought she'd take a lesson from Rick's video game. Maybe she wasn't yet sure what she planned to build, but she'd never be sorry she'd collected the materials.

MANO HADN'T SEEN HER husband in over twenty-four hours, but they had a standing date for happy hour. The Town Pump had one pool table and seating for ten. Dark wood paneling held the smell of cigarettes and stale beer. A stained-glass fixture above the single pool table read *Budweiser* in red, white, and blue, and the rest of the beer list was chalked onto a board behind the bar. It was Fri-day, near impossible to take a shot without knocking someone with the cue, but she and Rick persisted.

Mano called the 3 ball in the corner pocket but ended up sending the 5 into a side. Rick laughed and said, like he always did, "I
guess we'll count the slop."

She raised her glass to him, shook it so the ice rattled. When
she bent over the shot, she made sure her shirt dropped open at the
neck, an attempt to keep Rick's eyes focused on only her, but Rick
turned toward the bar. "I'll get us another round." His worn jeans
fit him perfectly, his shoulders were broad under his wool sweater.
She half loved him still, in spite of everything, which made her hate
him even more.

Rick was a near hero in town because he'd raised the alarm,
back in 1982, about the big flood in Rocky Mountain National
Park. He'd been deep in the park's high country early in the morning; right place, right time. Rick was cagey about the reasons,
always claimed the hand of God, and since the question of why
he was up there was both central to the story and somehow didn't
really matter, everyone let it go. It was Rick, after all, who called
in the flood in time to evacuate the downhill campgrounds and the
tourist district in Estes Park. If Rick hadn't been there, more than
three people would have died. Mano didn't believe for a minute that
God had anything to do with it. She was pretty sure Rick had been
poaching, or stealing antler sheds, or some shady nonsense, but still
the story had elevated Rick. It made him easier to fall in love with,
easier to forgive.

He'd been up near tree line, where the wind can strip a spruce
of half its foliage, can twist and bend the subalpine firs into flags,
when he heard a noise and thought *atom bomb*, thought *The world
is ending*, thought *Patrick Swayze in* Red Dawn*!* He searched for a
mushroom cloud, but saw instead rushing mud swallowing boulders, pulling trees out by their roots, different disaster, similar
effect. The flood, pulled by gravity, cleared everything in its path,
pulled boulders the size of humans, the size of cars, for miles before

dumping them in the alluvial fan below—the landscape forever altered. Rick had blocked the road, run for the emergency phone. "I just did what anyone would have done," Rick said, when he told the story, when people marveled at his decisive action.

"You going over to see that comet again tonight?" Rick asked. He leaned in and nibbled Mano's neck, and she wanted to pull away but didn't. He smelled like Old Spice, like the dusty heat of summer wind, and somehow the faintest whiff of rot, but it was earthy on Rick, pleasant, like the deep heart of a compost pile. As she breathed him in, she searched for the scent of whoever he'd been sleeping with, felt blood rushing to her head. She imagined another woman tracing her fingers along Rick's shoulder blade, thought of the way Rick's eyes turned tender in the moonlight, the love he'd once sworn to her whispered into some other woman's ear.

"You coming with me?" Mano held her breath but tried hard not to be obvious about it. Not that it mattered. Rick wasn't paying attention anyway.

Rick shook his head. "I'll just see you at home." It was a code and Mano knew it, and maybe what she had going on with Keith meant she had no right to hold other women against him, but she did. God, she did. And suddenly, more than anything, she wanted her sister. The night before her wedding, not quite a year ago, Ruth had pulled her into the backyard rock garden, an island of mossy flagstone and small boulders that bloomed from June through frost. She'd opened a bottle of whiskey, offered Mano the first shot.

"Your room here will stay yours. I know Rick's place doesn't have space for all your art mess." Ruth pointed to the small window of Mano's art room, a small space off the bedroom they'd all shared as girls, that Mano had shared, for a while, with Ruth's daughters. A large closet, really, but since the house usually held more family than it had rooms, nobody ever thought to use that space for clothes.

Mano's art room was the only place in the world that was hers alone. She'd built sculptures and mobiles from elk antlers, weathered driftwood, polished rocks, peach-tone seashells, sand dollars that rattled when she shook them and still carried the sweet-salted scent of the death of the creatures they'd once held. She'd filled presses with flowers she collected on mountain hikes, glued the flattened blooms around the edge of the window overlooking the side-yard garden. She had charcoal rubbings of bark patterns and gravestones. She hung bird feathers from string for close observation above an ink-stained table lit with shadeless lamps and candles so that she could vary the quality of the light. She'd posted silhouettes she'd done of her sisters and her best attempts at various calligraphy styles. Wall shelving sagged under the weight of watercolor tubes and oil paints and pastels and colored pencils and charcoals and brushes and solvents and glass baby food jars and old coffee cans full of gum erasers and pencil stubs. Her rock tumbler sat nearest the window, flanked on both sides by glass Mason jars full of tumbled glass in gold, greens, deep blues. In the past weeks, she'd filled every available space with trout. Pages she'd torn from art books and field guides. Her own sketches and Polaroids.

The room at Ruth's was a refuge she could run to, now or anytime, a gift she hadn't known she'd needed but Ruth, like a miracle, had. Ruth's ex, Del, showed up unannounced once or twice a year, made attempts to charm Ruth out of some money. It was easy to forget, in the face of all Ruth's determined self-sufficiency, how much she knew about the ways a heart could break. Ruth was busy, hovering, spider-like. Having spun herself an ample, sturdy web, Ruth spun relentlessly for all the people she loved.

"You're missing out, baby. Apparently, the comet has some sort of magic. Or poison. Some idiot thinks it's killing the fish." She felt the room spin, saw the red, white, and blue of the Budweiser lamp soften and swirl into the flashing lights of an emergency. Which it was, in a way, her last valiant effort to rescue her marriage. "Really, come with me."

Rick rolled his eyes. "Nope. I don't mind all your weird obsessions, Mano, but I don't want to get involved, either."

Mano found a stool, her heart straining against the tension in her chest. It had come out, after the flood, that the Army Corps of Engineers knew the dam was weak, had been announcing it, publicly, year after year. The park rangers had begged for repairs, for the funding it would take to shore it up. It had been easy for people who could not picture the scope of the coming catastrophe to ignore the early warnings from people who could. Rick was right about himself. He'd only ever done what anyone else would have, the day of the flood and every other day.

Rick cleared his half of the table easily. He turned away from the table before the 8 ball even dropped. She could see now that her marriage was over, that she should have understood this sooner. She could see also that nobody cared about the fish kills, about the water in her Pepsi bottle, about the facts of the world. Or they did, they knew, they saw, but they just weren't sure what to do.

Mano shoved her cue into his chest. "I think I will go see the comet," she said, even though that was no longer her plan. She swallowed her drink, glared at Rick, and tried hard not to wobble on her way out of the bar.

OUTSIDE, MANO LOOKED UP at the sky, overcast, fuzzy, no stars or comets to be seen. She walked the half mile from downtown to the riverbank in the silence and the dark. People loved the river, walked along it, fished from it, waded in it. She was amazed at what people were curious about, and what they weren't. She thought of Rick racing a flood down a mountain trail, praying the emergency phone would connect. She thought of the dead fish, the dim light of the maybe-comet. There was more than one way to sound an alarm.

Mano worked her way up the river, the water gurgling as it pushed against the rocks along its floor. Some of the fish were still floating, hung up on the twisted curl of protruding roots. The new-growth peachleaf willows were bright-yellow bare against the gray maze of cottonwood bark, nearly glowing in the hazed moonlight. Mano collected fallen branches, some as thick as her fist, others more delicate. She found a dead kingfisher next to a half-eaten trout, a few black feathers from crows or vultures. She swore to learn the difference. She collected a variety of river pebbles the size of large grapes. She dug in her purse for her pocketknife and the fishing line she'd swiped from Rick's truck.

The construction site was located about a mile west of town, not far from a heavily used section of trail that followed the river and the road between two city parks. At night, in the dark, it was deserted, though Mano thought the way the moonlight glowed blue behind the clouds, the way it backlit the dark thatches of woody branches, made it more beautiful now. She was the lone human moving in the world, but she was not alone—the woods full of wary animals who knew how to stay both invisible and watchful. Mano used the fishing wire to hang the thicker branches by both ends, like trapeze bars, just above eye level. She had to climb the trees a bit, shimmy awkwardly, belly down, out onto the limbs, but she managed to get the placement she was looking for. She rolled a larger rock around for a stool and started hanging the corpses.

From one branch, she hung five dead trout, some by their tails, some by their gills. The moonlight reflected off the fish scales, lit the wet of the fish skin into a brilliant shine. She rushed together a series of fishing line macramé that she draped around tree trunks and limbs, filled with river-polished rocks. From another branch, Mano hung a single trout with crow feathers attached so that they radiated in all directions like night-black rays, and next to that, the dead kingfisher, strung up by each of its wings so that it looked bat-like in the shadows, nearly vampiric.

The dead animals and rocks hung at eye level, lifted so that the men could no longer look down on them. Impossible now for people to miss the horror of what they'd done. Mano lay down on the damp earth of the riverbank, tracked the moon's trajectory across the night sky, observed the shifting light against the terrible beauty of her sculpture. She squinted into the darkness, hoping she'd see the comet clearly, tail and all, but saw nothing. She felt achingly, utterly, alone.

SOMETIME JUST BEFORE DAWN, Mano made it to Ruth's, crawled onto the hidden trundle mattress she kept underneath her art desk, and fell asleep. She slept through to afternoon, woke with a pounding headache. Downstairs, Ruth was at the kitchen table with a ham and Swiss sandwich, a coffee mug, a Mason jar full of homemade sweet pickles. The evening newspaper and a hand of solitaire were spread in front of her.

Mano felt a bit ashamed of herself. "Four o'clock already? I'm surprised you didn't get me up earlier." She got a coffee cup from the shelf, grateful for Ruth's odd hours, the house perpetually full of fresh coffee, a bottomless pot.

"Rick called," Ruth said. She raised an eyebrow, then looked down at her cards. "And Keith."

Mano sat across from her. Ruth added a generous pour of Irish cream to her coffee, then Mano's, her face lined with concern. "Listen, Mano, the only good I got from my marriage was the kids, but divorce hasn't exactly been a picnic, either. Just be sure you know what you're hoping for, okay?"

Ruth's unexpected kindness brought tears, and Mano let them

run down her cheeks in rivers, let the snot drip from her nose like rain off a roof, let her shoulders shake in deep sobs. She felt sorry for herself, mostly, but also for the Stevies, for the dead kingfisher. She wondered again whether Ruth knew that Rick was cheating too, that he'd been cheating first.

Ruth sniffed and pushed the newspaper toward Mano. "When you pull yourself together, maybe you want to explain this?"

Mano wiped her eyes on her sleeve and then her nose, too. The front page of the newspaper had a grainy black-and-white photo of the construction site on the river, her fish drooping from their branches, the kingfisher, half eaten by some scavenger, attached by only one wing. She felt a quick shiver of excitement—that other people would see what she saw, that she would no longer be alone in seeing it.

The article, though, was full of speculation and outrage, her sculpture interpreted as bizarre satanic ritual, possibly related to fears of Halley's Comet. The reporter quoted a number of residents who hadn't thought it possible that depravity of that level could exist in their town. "Why would anyone kill a kingfisher?" one outraged resident asked. "Them cutthroat are endangered," another said. "And they already been struggling this season." Higher than usual numbers of dead fish had been observed in and near the river this spring, the article read, causing many to speculate that Halley's Comet had somehow upset the balance of the river ecosystem, though the reporter was careful to add that the cause of the fish kills was unknown and unproven. "Whoever did this should be tarred and feathered," said a final interviewee, who added that she no longer felt safe to walk her corgis along the river trail. "Or at least they should know better. People are scared enough."

Mano thought back to her favorite art professor, a woman who wore colorful patterned caftans and Birkenstocks, kind and creative and cool. "You can't follow your art into the world to defend it," she'd said. "Your art has to speak for itself." Mano was horrified. This was not at all what she'd thought her art would say.

Ruth studied the photo in the paper, a smile pulling at the corners of her mouth. "The crow feathers? On the fish? I like that. That's got style."

Mano tried to sort her thoughts into some sort of order—her marriage, the comet, the way the world was, the way the world should be, but it was like untangling knotted hair, complicated, painful, time-consuming. "I didn't kill the kingfisher. I didn't kill anything." Her whole body felt shaky, loose, impossible to contain. She stood up and paced the length of the kitchen.

She grabbed the Pepsi bottle out of her purse, handed it to Ruth. "It's from the river. It's a sample. If I get it tested, I can prove that the construction poisoned the fish."

"The fish are dead in the river for everyone to see," Ruth said, shaking her head. "And nobody else is asking why."

Mano felt the truth of that settle all around her. Knowing why carried a weight—a responsibility to act or the shame of not having acted. So many things were easier not to know. "So what do I do now?"

She wanted Ruth to weigh in, give her the answer, say exactly the right thing. Ruth might have been late to mothering Mano, but she'd come on strong over the past ten years, lumping Mano into the same category as her children. It was easy to believe that Ruth saw the best next step, always. Mano felt hope dissipate the pressure that was building inside her body. Maybe she wasn't as alone as she felt.

"I can't tell you what to do about this." Ruth looked sorry. She made eye contact, set her cards down.

"You tell me what to do all the time. And what not to do." Mano's laugh caught the throat phlegm from all her crying, and she half choked.

"Too bad you didn't ask me about this dead animal sculpture," Ruth said, smiling. "I would have given a real clear no on that one."

"I think I'm going to call Keith." Mano savored Ruth's shocked expression. It tasted sweet, this openness, like some sort of freedom.

"Think twice before you do anything stupid," Ruth said. She tilted her head to the side, tapped her index finger on the newspaper photo. Her face was loving. Understanding. "Anything else, I mean."

Mano didn't know which of her choices, past or future, she'd end up regretting the most. But Ruth's coffee, her pickles, her Lorna Doone cookies, her judgment, her presence, had become part of the shelter of the house. Mano felt it solidify something underneath and inside her.

KEITH'S BACKYARD WAS A revelation. He planned to start a business growing native plants for yards and gardens. He'd turned his half-acre lot into an experimental low-water landscape, had built himself a small greenhouse for breeding native seed. "They know there isn't near enough water for all the people about to move in around here, and the lawns are an absolute disaster, water-wise. Anyway, they call it 'xeriscaping,' landscaping to save water. Pretty sure there's a future in it."

Mano, knowing how much Ruth loved her peonies and her tulips, how much time and effort she put into her Kentucky bluegrass, doubted the solvency of his plan. "If I wanted to live in a desert," Ruth would say, "I'd have stayed in Nevada," and so Mano was only half listening as Keith droned on about plants—columbine and manzanita, grama grass and waxflower—all grown from seed he'd collected in the wild. She considered the best way to interrupt him. He'd be more open to her ideas if she was naked, but she decided to keep her clothes on.

"We have to tell people about the fish kills," she said, cutting off a passionate monologue about breeding for drought tolerance. "Call the state regulators. The newspaper."

Keith shook his head. "Lloyd would know it was us."

"Lloyd is already going to hell. We might as well go right with him if we let this go on." Keith wouldn't meet her eyes. He knew he was taking the wrong side. She'd already lost.

"I can't risk my job over some fish, Mano. You shouldn't either. Lloyd says it's not harmful to people or anything. Like there's not enough of whatever the chemical is to poison a whole human."

Mano set her face to the wind so that the tears in her eyes could be for anything or nothing at all. She took deep, slow breaths. She tried to match the pace of her own breathing to the movement of the linden branches in the gusts. As a young girl, she used to pretend to call Ruth and Teresa on a toy phone that had a working rotary dial. *Come back*, she'd tell them, *come home*. After a while, she'd realized that painting was a less lonely way to talk to herself. Looking at Keith just then, seeing all the ways he would never listen to her, she realized it still was.

"I haven't had any luck seeing this comet," Keith said. "All this goddamn cloud cover."

"Well, it's up there," Mano said. If there was no more Rick, and no more Keith, if her life was now her own again, and of course it was, who else had it ever belonged to, then she could be certain about what to do next.

Mano went back to Ruth's and called the paper, told them everything she knew and some things she suspected, that Lloyd was covering up for the construction company, that the regulators had not been called. Her next call was to Lloyd himself. "You'll want to fire me soon enough anyway," she said, "so to save both of us the trouble, I'll just quit." Ruth made bottomless pots of coffee, gloated in insufferable ways when she beat Mano in double

solitaire, gave her the number of a good divorce attorney. *Drop Rick.*
Mano did not return Keith's calls. *Drop Keith.*

Weeks later, the paper finally ran an article about the fish
kills, except they only wrote about one, as though it had only happened one time. The article was sympathetic to the construction
company—an investigation had shown that all the required mit-
igations were in place, made the chemical spills that dropped the
river pH so much it killed the fish seem like something mild and
inevitable, a regrettable but ultimately harmless mistake. Lloyd
was highlighted with a reassuring quote, "The fish we put in the
tank the next day lived, are still alive. Whatever was in the river, it
was a very temporary state. It flowed away as quickly as it flowed
in." Various state and local authorities had collaborated to find
nothing—no systemic problem with construction near the river,
no lingering negative environmental effects. Lloyd and Keith were
commended for their quick-thinking actions to preserve the integ-
rity of the city's drinking water.

Mano took down all the trout she'd painted before and started
again, painting trout over and over on postcard stock—trout swim-
ming above the rocky peaks across the Estes Valley, trout spawning
in a native waxflower grove in full spring bloom, trout wiggling
through the geometric beauty of a spiderweb, trout shooting like
comets through a maze of peachleaf willow growth, their spots
shining like stars on a dark summer night. She sent these postcards
to her congresspeople, to the mayor, to the governor, all with pleas
for species protection, for water quality, for oversight and repara-
tions. Most of the officials declined to reply, but Mano kept writing,
kept painting, kept offering chances.

The Best Response to Fear

⸺

EVERY DAY BEFORE SHE left for work, Amy boiled coffee on the wood-burning stove Bobby Jackson had rigged from a fifty-gallon oil drum and read the newspaper that still appeared, like some kind of magic, in the driveway. It had been months since they'd had the money to pay for the subscription. He couldn't explain it.

"We're in luck, baby," she'd say, folding the pages neatly, saving the paper to shred and crumple under the stove kindling later. "The recession is over!" Amy said this every day, a joke between them. Bobby would laugh briefly, rattle his fingertips against the plastic taped over the broken windows, lean the military surplus cots they slept on now against the wall like Murphy beds.

"I do feel lucky," he'd say, and Amy would laugh, set a cup of coffee in front of him as he sat in a foldable chair at their foldable card table. She'd stand next to him, pull his head into her belly, tangle her fingers in the curls of his hair, hair he was letting grow now. One good thing about his new life is that he could get scruffy, go full hairy werewolf if he wanted, and he wouldn't have to take

shit from the other guys at work. *Gone hippie*, they used to say if he
went too long between haircuts. *You trying to look like a Q-tip or what?*

They'd been living in the old office building on the east side
of the sugar mill property since the foreclosure, the decorative tin
ceiling tiles tinged with green, the cracked plaster and lath walls
lined with shelves of old Mason jars, some blue, some clear, all full
of odd powders and residues, cobwebs, dead spiders. Bobby's parents, Elmer and Marcia, had offered them his boyhood room, but
they'd asked instead to move into the decaying sugar mill property
Elmer bought at auction years ago. It felt somehow more digni-
fied to live alone, let them pretend that they were still independent
thirty-somethings, that the life they'd built for themselves hadn't
caught fire, burned to ash. Sunlight leaked through the yellowed
curtains every morning, but by afternoon the place was all shadow,
the light blocked by the six towering silos, still the tallest structures
in town. Any day now, he was sure, he'd wake to find Amy folding
her clothes, packing them neatly into an old milk crate.

You're lucky I lasted as long as I did, she'd say, gesturing from one
side of the room to the other. *This shit.*

But Amy still kissed his forehead on her way out the door,
flashed a brilliant smile, said something to make him laugh, "Chin
up, jackass," or some version of their wedding vows, "For richer and
poorer." Ten years into their marriage, Bobby knew every one of
her smile lines, the way emotion morphed and shifted them. They
betrayed her, revealed the true feelings she hid behind her brave
face. Bobby knew she pictured, as he did sometimes, the granite
countertops in their old kitchen, the Jacuzzi tub he'd installed for
her on their fifth anniversary, the way the foreclosure notice had
flapped and chattered with the breeze. There was no way to see so
much loss as some grand adventure. It wasn't a human response.

There were two large outbuildings at the mill, one a skeleton,
exposed, surrounded by piles of bricks where the walls had already

crumbled away. The other still had its walls, doors he could lock, treasures to mine: rusted backhoes, trailers, old vehicles, dented metal lockers, beet crates. He'd seen this as an opportunity and filed an LLC on a garage of his own. Because it was all he could afford, Bobby put a spray-painted sign out by the road. *Engines. Alignments. Oil Changes. Fair Prices.*

Weeks passed and nobody came, and Bobby knew why. When times were tough, people learned to change their own damn oil. He spent his days reading the names of beet harvesters and plant workers listed in old handwritten payroll books, 1901–1938, paging through records of layoffs from Great Western's bankruptcy in the 1980s, name after name of hard-luck blue-collar guys from recessions past. He could conjure them if he wanted to. Ghosts with boots that needed resoling. Ghosts with coveralls worn to threads.

Amy was still working, home health aide, part time. She'd gotten a referral recently and her hours were up. Bobby knew he should be grateful but he wasn't quite. Just because he knew jealousy was ugly didn't mean he could stop feeling it. Being with Amy had always been like that, like all the available luck was pulled into orbit around her, like her gravity was stronger than everyone else's. Amy's scratch tickets always paid at least five dollars. Amy always caught the most fish from the quarry ponds. When Amy found coins on the sidewalk, they were always heads up. He hadn't ever, in their old life, been jealous of Amy's luck, and now it somehow helped to remind himself that even Amy's luck had been no match against the forces of the global economy. Amy had lost the house too, same as he had.

Bobby sometimes climbed into Amy's cot, pulled her blankets up over his head, breathed in the smell of her—spring snow crabapple trees, river water on sun-baked granite. The room felt less haunted when he imagined her in it. His heart rate would slow, the chaos in his head calm a bit, and he could pretend they hadn't lost so much, stop worrying that his marriage might be a fair-weather deal. When he'd emerge, un-cocoon himself, the glass Mason jars would catch the sunlight, reflect it back at him like hundreds of eyes, each one a bright shining accusation:

You are in bed while your wife is at work.

Some days, Bobby could force himself up off the cot, make a few phone calls, try to drum up some business. Most days, though, he pulled the blanket back over his head.

"I'd be at work if there was any," he'd say, and then, "Get out of my head, ghosts."

MAYBE THE PAPERS SAID the worst of the recession was over, but Bobby couldn't see it in real life, in the darkened downtown storefronts and liquidation sales, the hopeless expressions of the people sleeping in used cars in the Walmart parking lot, in the still-crowded foreclosure auctions. It had not been made clear to Bobby whether he'd been fired from his job as lead mechanic at the Saturn dealership because the economy tanked, or because GM wanted to kill the brand, or because he'd called in hungover one too many times. The occasional sick day had not been a problem before the recession. He'd eventually decided that the reason wasn't as important as the results. Days passed. He tried to look forward. Every morning he'd call Bruce, who had a construction company, a whole fleet of trucks, and every morning Bruce said some variation of the same thing. *No, thanks, we're still barely working anyway, everything's still stalled.*

"Really man," Bruce had said, the last time he'd checked in. "I'll call you."

Amy, back from work, sat down next to him in the shade of the giant silos. Bobby had spent most of the afternoon cleaning the bricks from the collapsed walls. He could disintegrate the old

mortar with his bare fingers, watch it fall away, dissipate into the
soil. It gave him some sort of hope, the tidy stacks of clean bricks
next to the chaotic pile of collapsed wall.

"What you doing, baby?" Amy asked. She picked up a brick,
held it close, inspected it closely.

"Thought I'd clean things up a bit," Bobby said. "Give myself
something to do."

Amy looked up from the brick, inspecting him just as closely.
"Still nothing, eh?"

No matter how she meant it, Bobby heard it both ways—still
nothing, as in no work, and still nothing as in not working, not
contributing, worthless. Amy put a hand on his knee, rubbed with
her thumb, and Bobby felt his skin warm under her touch. "Maybe
we need a bigger sign out front? Maybe we can get a banner made,
something more professional?" Bobby loved the hope in Amy's
mouth, would take whatever small proof that she still believed in
him, which was the only way he could see believing in himself.

They heard the chug of a diesel engine, saw Elmer fiddling with
the chain of the mill gate, Marcia waving from the passenger seat.

"My parents tell you they were stopping by?" When Bobby
stood up, the pea gravel crunched under his feet, shifting, unstable.
He grabbed both Amy's hands, steadied himself against her weight,
helped her to standing.

"I'm always happy to see them." Amy brushed the dirt off her
pants first, then his.

Marcia, her hair still honey-brown, untied and a bit wild in the
wind, offered Amy a foil-wrapped package, handed Bobby four
quart jars. "Krautburgers and applesauce," she said, and Bobby
pictured his mother's kitchen counters as they'd always been in
fall—covered in cabbage cores, scattered with stray flour, an apple
pie still steaming from the oven, the kitchen air heavy with cinnamon sugar and brassica funk. "I'll do another round, next week."

"City sent a notice about the weeds," Elmer said. "Makes me think they're going to follow through on what they've been threatening, declare the place blight." Elmer wore jeans stained with motor oil and ditch mud, suspenders over a T-shirt, a fancy welder's cap. Marcia made Elmer a fancy stitch cap every year at Christmas, and Elmer wore it every day, welding or not. Elmer's sun-worn skin was contracting, squeezing, tightening him into himself, making him take up less space in the world with every passing year. Bobby felt the same was happening to him, even though he was only thirty-six, even though there were not yet any visible markers. The recession had him pinned like a vise, his skin stretched too tight over his bones.

"Blight nothing," Amy said. "I've always loved this place. Even before." Bobby surveyed the grounds—piles of brick from crumbled walls, peeling paint and cracked wooden siding, puncture vine and purple loosestrife sprouting from the cracks in the concrete ramps. It had seen better days. It would have been easier to love in its prime.

"That's the spirit," Elmer said. He pulled Marcia into an up-tempo waltz right there on the pea gravel. "This place is our retirement fund, honey. It's all we got worth anything." Elmer was an odd duck, legendary for impromptu jigs, occasional outbursts of singing.

"You can't spend property, old man," Marcia said, but she laughed, let him spin her across the gravel.

Bobby envied Elmer his lightness of heart, envied the way everyone, Marcia, Amy, accepted his dad's odd quirks and habits. Elmer could decide he was going to eat fire instead of dinner, Bobby thought, and both Amy and Marcia would be delighted by his innovative thinking. Bobby felt he'd lost the trick of joy, could no longer conjure happiness.

"If I heat these up," Amy said, "can you two stay for dinner?"

Marcia and Elmer were having their own hard times, the recession having come for them like it had come for everyone. Still, Marcia would fill her own freezer and theirs with doughy rolls stuffed with ground beef, black pepper, cabbage. They'd have shelves full of jars—apple pie filling, pickled beets, green beans and corn. Amy, who believed in good company, that time spent together was a powerful expression of love, would insist on regular family meals.

"Let me help you." Marcia took the applesauce back from Bobby, and Bobby watched as the women walked close to one another, smiling. He envied them this easy affection, wished he understood the magic of these women, of Elmer, for that matter, the light they all shone into dark places. He worried again about the deepening lines in Amy's face. He wondered where Amy's seemingly boundless good humor ended, where Marcia's did. He wanted to know where the limit was, how to see the line of too much to ask, how in God's creation Elmer had managed to stay on the right side of it all these years. He felt near desperate to learn this lesson before it was too late.

"You poked around much in these buildings?" Elmer drew him back into the moment.

"Yeah, some. There's a lot to look through."

Elmer nodded. "Even I don't know all this place holds, but I got something to show you."

There was a small cinder-block outbuilding at the back of the property, two manual garage doors, padlocked shut, multiple windows cracked or broken. Bobby hadn't made it back here, had spent most of his scavenging time in the larger mill building. Elmer unlocked the doors and handed Bobby the keys. Dust swirled in the fading sunlight, and underneath some crates of rusted engine parts and old oil cans was the unmistakable shape of a Ford Falcon in baby blue, a white stripe on each side, front to back.

"That car was really something, in its day," Elmer said. He was shifting again, one leg to another, almost on tiptoes, a joyful shuffle. "Thought your mom and I could be your first customers."

Bobby felt his eyes well up. It was too much, this parental charity. It felt like something dangerous, though Bobby couldn't even tell himself why. He ran his hand along the Falcon.

Elmer stopped shuffling, furrowed his brow. "Unless you got something else lined up, of course."

Bobby knew Elmer knew he didn't. What Bobby wanted were jobs that didn't come from Elmer, or through him, but he couldn't turn any job down, so he worked to master the lump in his throat. "Of course, Dad. It's a great car."

"You get me an estimate, okay? We're paying."

Bobby pushed both hands into his forehead, tried to pull the skin tight. "No, Dad, that's too much. Just let me do it."

A V-formation of geese flew overhead, heading east, not south, their insistent honking a tremendous racket.

"You think those geese are just temporarily confused?" Bobby asked.

"Huh?"

"Do you think they're just flying east, like, today? Like they're going to stop off in Johnstown for whatever reason and then head south? Or has something messed with their instinct and they've forgotten, completely, that they're supposed to go south?" Bobby wondered about instinct. Was it magic or science, the way a goose knew when it was time to move on, the way a goose knew which direction to go?

"Geese don't forget shit," Elmer said. "They just go south or they don't."

Bobby nodded. "Dad, I appreciate this, I do. I just worry that I'll never get back to wiping my own ass, you know?"

Elmer put a hand on his shoulder. "Ridiculous. It's just a rough patch, son. They come and they go." Bobby didn't say anything, so Elmer clapped his shoulder a few times. "We better get in for dinner."

They walked toward the office Amy had turned into their home. The mountains, so close to sunset, had turned a deeper shade of blue than the sky.

BOBBY HAD GONE INSOMNIAC with worry. Nights, he sang along to Freddy Fender and the Texas Tornados, sometimes listened to Coast to Coast AM for the alien sightings, the true ghost stories, the theories about Quantitative Easing and the printing of money that weren't so different from those he heard on NPR during the day. Bobby couldn't square it, but he loved to imagine himself with the powers of the Fed—conjuring his missing mortgage payments out of thin air, piling stacks of bills on some banker's desk. Instead, he worked on the Falcon, patching the tires, replacing the fuel line. He found a sort of Zen in the work, an avoidance of his own mind. He was good at diagnosis, at repair, his skills an exact match to those the recession had devalued.

He'd scavenged some parts from the junk piles, given others a good cleaning when he would usually have thrown them out. He thought about all the different things the word *recession* could mean—smooth beaches in low tide, off-grid houses with solar panels and composting toilets, hearts like ships shrinking against the horizon, drifting inevitably away from each other. He sometimes set the tools down for a minute or two, exhaustion sweeping over him, everything he lifted heavier than it actually was.

Amy came into the garage with two cups of coffee, handed one to him, and he marveled again at the million small gifts she managed to give. She leaned against the Falcon, the steam from her coffee rising to her face. "How's it going in here?"

"You ever think what we'll do if nobody but Mom and Dad give me a car to fix?"

"Give it time, Bobby," she said. "It's not like all the other mechanics are thriving. Nobody has money for anything. Everyone is just . . . waiting, I guess."

"Can't wait forever." *If I could just invent work the way the government invents money*, Bobby thought to say, but he decided to keep quiet.

"Yeah, I hear you." Amy tossed her hair, brought her mug to her mouth with both hands cupped around it. "I guess I keep hoping something bigger is going to give. That it's true what the papers say, that the recession is over, that the work is going to come back."

Bobby swore, let a fist drop on the side of the Falcon, saw Amy startle and jump, saw her brow furrow, her eyes reflect his anger back at him. "I don't see how that shit's helping, Bobby." She looked at the ceiling, her face reddening, her eyes welling. "I keep trying to make the best of all of this, to keep both our spirits up, and you're just . . . I mean, I love you, Bobby, but you aren't doing any of the work."

Bobby felt his gut burning, felt his limbs weaken. He knew it. He'd been afraid of this for so long. Still, all he had to offer her was a flimsy defense. He pointed to the Falcon. "There is no work but this, Amy. What is it you want from me?"

Her anger made her hair shine, her eyes flash, her beauty flare so brilliant that he moved toward her just as she moved away. "That's not the work I'm talking about. That's not even close."

He let her walk away then, heard the spin of tires on gravel fade until he heard nothing, until he was alone with the echoes of Amy. He sat down on a cinder block, felt tears prickle the back of his eyes, and through the world gone wobbly he saw the ghosts again. Men with lined faces sweeping the floors. Men stacking beet crates. Men arriving with their harvests, hoping to God the mill would pay them fair.

Bobby retreated, as he did so often, to Amy's cot, but he was too rattled to settle. Her blankets were like ornamentals in bloom, straight springtime, and the reflection of the rising moon in the Mason jars were all Amy: Amy laughing on the top of a mountain trail, Amy lying naked in the bedroom of their foreclosed house, Amy smiling on their wedding day, her face turned toward the sunshine.

BOBBY WAS RESTLESS, ROAMING the south side of the silo block predawn, throwing rocks at rabbits. He had a .22 inside but he didn't feel like going back to the old office building to get it. The impotent chain-link fence he'd rigged around the garden had not been any kind of deterrent to the rabbits, nor had the flashing metallic ribbons he'd tied to small stakes so they'd dance and snap in the wind. They had eaten his fall crop lettuce and spinach down to stubs. He was a quarter mile from the road but heard traffic anyway. The road was usually busy, a direct line to the main highway, but not at this time of morning. Two police cars drove past.

He let his body relax after a full, tensing shiver, took aim, and hit the rabbit square, killing it instantly. Not that there was much of a trick to that, given the rabbits' fear response. It took a pretty poor shot to miss a rabbit frozen in place under a sulfur light in the middle of an open driveway, and Bobby had been honing his aim since he'd been living in the mill. Bobby knew rabbits were stupid that way—the best response to fear is controlled action, not paralysis. But he understood it, too. It took effort to keep moving when there was no visible destination, when it felt like something large was stalking you, like the unfortunate end of everything approached, wrapped in destiny, absolute.

They hadn't started eating the rabbits because they liked the flavor, exactly. It's just things had gotten so lean, and there were rabbits everywhere. Amy stopped at the store after work, bought paprika, peppers, dried pintos, and they ate the stew together over rice, listening to the radio, which was still, like some sort of miracle, free. Bobby got used to the gamey flavor of rabbit stew quickly, came to appreciate the way the stringy tendons caught between his teeth. It had taken Amy three attempts at the recipe before she could eat the rabbit without gagging.

"Hot sauce saves the day," she'd said finally, grimacing.

"Look, we don't have to eat the rabbits," he said. "We could just get a ham hock or something."

"Maybe not," Amy said. "But it's all part of the frugality game, right?"

"What?" Bobby asked.

"The post-recession survival game," Amy said. "It's like we get poor-people virtue points for any crazy we teach ourselves to tolerate. Like eating rabbits out of the yard just because they're free."

Bobby had run his hand over Amy's shoulder and down her back, his fingers caressing her shoulder blades, his mind a panic of wings in a graceful, frantic migration, his hands searching for a tether. He thought of the misery they'd endured: the missing mortgage payments, the months of wondering how long it would take the bank to come for them, whether they'd take the house in February, in May, in September, the neighbors watching out their windows. Amy had taken it all in stride. Only now could he see the traces of bitterness on her characteristic light heart.

Now, he saw Amy, backlit by the sunrise, walking toward him. He caught a whiff of rabbit before he could see what she was carrying, and he knew she'd found the skins he'd been curing on a rack in one of the sheds.

When she was close enough that he could see the worry in

her eyes, she handed the pelt to him. "What's your plan for these, Bobby?" she asked, her nose wrinkled even as she ran her fingers through one of the furs, touching it in a way they had stopped touching each other.

"Thought I'd make a coat," Bobby answered.

Amy looked at him for a long time, as though she was deciding how serious he was, how concerned she had to be. She took a deep breath. She took one of his hands. "Babe. Be cool. A blanket, maybe."

Bobby thought then that it did seem a bit much, a coat handmade from rabbit skins. He'd be likely to wear it even when he wasn't at the mill, and then what? He'd felt for a while now that his instincts about how to live had gone wobbly, that he was drifting slowly out of the community, caught in a riptide of ever-developing eccentricities, interrupted in becoming whatever it was he was going to become, the Great Recession and his own bad choices reacting like the baking soda and 7Up of his third-grade science project, either thing on its own benign, uninteresting, but erupting in combination, leaving a sticky coating all over his life, flies buzzing and biting. It took so much effort to do even simple things, to just exist. He wanted to bounce back, to believe in an inevitable recovery, but the world did not feel particularly elastic.

Amy surprised him then, put both her arms around his shoulders, pulled herself close to him, and he held her around her waist, closed his eyes, felt the heat of her breath spread across his neck. He let the rabbit skin drop to the ground.

Amy pulled back, made eye contact. "Bobby," she said, "you keep making all this into something it's not, like it's the end of everything, like we'll never recover, and I can't . . . I'm going to need you to buck up a little, okay?"

"I'll try, Amy. Really I will." Bobby pulled her into a close embrace then, caught the flash of the metal roof of the processing building behind her, brief, lovely, light like the spark of Elmer's old arc welder, the kind of light Bobby knew better than to look at directly, beauty that could sear his retinas. He felt the warmth of his wife pass clothes to skin, skin to muscle, muscle to bone, bone to cells, and he felt himself absorbent, porous, greedy for more.

BOBBY HAD GONE BACK to the last days of the Falcon project focused, calmed by a new sense of control. He saw the whole job, his next steps and the steps to come, lay themselves out in front of him. He just needed to get this car running and other cars would follow, and all the locks of his life would start to release, and everything that had been closed would open. He'd accepted that even if there was some sort of Quantitative Easing process for conjuring luck, it would be just like the cash the Fed printed during the recession, the lucky people getting all the new luck just like the rich people were somehow getting all the new money. He didn't have to use that as any kind of measuring stick for his own life, didn't need to measure his worth at all so much as remember it, touch it from time to time, protect it in the deep core of himself.

When Marcia saw the Falcon, when Elmer started it up, she winked at Bobby. "Sharp car," she said. "Let's cruise."

Amy held his hand in the backseat, her body close to his. They drove past the gnarled cottonwoods between the quarry ponds and the river, the leaves so yellowed that the slightest breeze liberated them from the tree, sent them trembling in whirling spirals, first away from the trunk, then down to the roots. Elmer found Marty Robbins on the radio, sang along as they headed west toward the foothills, all four windows open to the bluest of big skies, the cumulus-puffy promise of a sun-bright October day.

Sister Agnes Mary in the
Spring of 2012

IN THE VESTIBULE OF St. Paul's Catholic Church, set off from the main sanctuary, tiny flames shimmer inside blood-red votive holders. There are shelves and shelves of them. The smell of matches and candle wax and the vague remnants of Sunday's incense make the air feel rich, tangibly holy. Sister Agnes Mary, age seventy-four, has risen early every morning for over fifty years to pray in this vestibule. She prays with her mother's old rosary, worrying the beads—magnesite, amethyst—between her fingers. For years, her morning prayers were full of gratitude for the routines of her life, happy prayers, full of certainty and light, fresh air in the stale sanctuary. Those prayers wandered and spread, rose as though drawn by a magnet toward heaven, escaped through stained glass.

Yesterday, when Sister discovered that the church planned to approve a new oil and gas drill site just behind the playground at

St. Paul's Catholic Primary School, she went directly to the new priest, Father Morel, with her opposition. Father Morel, a grim liturgical leader, recently arrived from Argentina. He is twenty-eight years old, but his youth does not translate, as she hoped it might, into progressive thought.

"It's too close to the children, Father," she said. "They won't be able to—"

Father Morel put a hand on her shoulder. Sister felt it as though he'd placed it over her mouth. "There is nothing to worry about, Sister," he said, smiling the same smile Sister had given to the kindergartners she used to teach, condescension dressed up as kindness. "And if you persist in worry, lift your worry up to God."

Sister could feel him looking past her, as though she had already gone to join the saints. Sister thought to snap her fingers in his face, poke one of his eyes, make him certain of her still-living presence in the world through some madcap Laurel-and-Hardy-style violence. Instead, she stared at the stained-glass windows behind him. One portrayed the Virgin Mary kneeling at the base of the cross in submissive, sorrowful prayer. Another depicted Mary serene, cradling a swaddled babe. Sister had been praying the glorious mysteries on the rosary, deep into the coronation of the Virgin. Sister prefers the Mary of Revelation—pregnant belly rounded like the moon under her feet, twelve stars shining in her hair, defying the demon dragon that intends to eat her newborn infant. Sister has never seen Revelation Mary in stained glass.

Sister knows better than Father Morel about the possible harms of the drilling project. The church supported Sister through a PhD in ecology when she was a novitiate, and then it asked her to spend her lifetime as a kindergarten teacher, tying shoelaces and zippering jackets, which she did without complaint, which she came to truly love. Now, her aching joints burn despite the pillow she places between them and the wooden kneeler. She has belonged to her order, to the church, to God, and she once found solace in that belonging, was ever obedient to it. Now she struggles with what, exactly, her faith demands, how to behave when she suspects that God's laws and the church's laws are not an exact match.

Mano, Sister's younger blood sister by eight years, arrives and kneels on her right side. Mano's hair is wind-tousled, spruce-scented. Ruth, Sister's other blood sister, a year older than Sister herself, kneels on her left. Ruth smells like burnt toast. Her sisters often meet her for morning prayers, and Sister is glad for their company. There are no other nuns left at St. Paul's—some have died, some have moved to convalescent homes, one is in prison for writing Bible verses in blood on nuclear warheads after breaking into a secure facility. Sister has always seen this last act as vanity, action to get attention more than action to do good, but now she feels more confused than certain. She doesn't know whether a lifetime of prayers for a broken world, prayers she has fervently delivered, is sufficient. Her prayers have become heavy with her doubt.

"Father Morel," Ruth says, "is planning to let John March put a gas drill rig on the vacant lot behind the school."

Ruth likes to be first with the news. Sister is fine allowing this.

"Right there behind the playground?" Mano asks. "So close to the children?"

"These ridiculous men," Sister says, shaking her head, "and their nonsense ideas."

"Fracking," Ruth says. It sounds like spitting. Ruth has long been suspicious of the increased air pollution from fracking in town, tells Sister and Mano stories she hears of miscarriages, still-births, preemies that fit in the palm of someone's hand. Ruth is a retired labor and delivery nurse, has delivered half the population of Greeley, Colorado. Sister taught kindergarten to the Catholic ones. Sister loved those children, loves her sisters' children, loves all children. Mano painted landscapes and portraiture for money, built found-object sculptures for art. Now retired, the sisters drink coffee, play gin rummy, volunteer a few hours a week.

"We should call our senators," Mano says. Mano is their activist. Member of the Sierra Club. Avid reader of Rachel Carson and Edward Abbey. "Make signs. Picket the corners."

Ruth pokes Sister in the ribs, then points toward the ceiling. "What does your husband have to say?" Ruth means God, of course. She likes to tease Sister. It's lighthearted, this teasing. Ruth's love language.

Sister shrugs. "Man of few words," she says. Mano and Ruth giggle.

"The silent treatment," Mano says. "Sounds like all three of my marriages."

"Maybe he thinks that after all these years he shouldn't have to tell you what to do," Ruth says. "Maybe he thinks you should just know."

"Well I don't. It's maddening." Sister detangles the beads from her fingers, wraps them loosely around her wrist instead. Her sisters are having fun. She tries to relax.

Mano nods. "That exact kind of maddening caused two of my three divorces."

"She can't divorce God," Ruth says.

Her sisters look directly at her. Their dresses rustle. Their shifting weight makes the old kneelers settle and pop.

"You two," Sister says, "are really snagging my knits." This makes all three of them laugh, their departed mother's favorite way to chastise them.

Sister returns to her knees and to the rosary. She keeps the Book of Revelation clear in her mind's eye—Mother Mary sprouting eagle's wings to escape the beast, riding the thermals above the solace desert. Mary stalwart, borne by her solitary strength and faith. Mary rewarded.

SISTER WRAPS A SCARF around her ears, bundles herself into a black woolen coat that hangs to her knees. It is two in the morning. She can see her breath in the near-frost chill, and the air soothes the constant arthritic ache in her joints, like fire doused to smoldering embers. Above the rooftops of the ranch houses, Sister can see the flare stacks of new gas wells burning. If she spins where she's standing, she can see five burning flares, but she knows there are hundreds, maybe thousands, in her county alone. They don't smell like anything unless she stands right underneath them. Close up, Sister smells engine grease, animal offal, wet clay—the bowels of the earth and the chemicals that strip them wafting together after the burn. Above the actual flames, the fumes and the heat distort the view, a world scrambled into waves, unrecognizable. Beyond that space, the chemicals are swallowed by the big-sky atmosphere and become invisible, which makes it easy to forget that they are still there.

She carries two gallons of bleach in a heavy canvas tote bag, and the pain in her shoulders and neck begins to spread down into her forearms, her fingers and hands, and then even her heart and her belly radiate the ache. Tonight, Sister will execute a plan she's been working out for days. She hopes it will bring her close again to God. She worries it might push him further away. She notes the absence of direct answer to her prayers, contemplates the obvious lack of instructive miracle. She is grateful for the internet, for the wealth of information available to even an aging nun, the ways the invisibility of age might shield and protect her, the ways it might be a veiled, sharp-edged gift. Floodlights illuminate the playground— the swing set, the spiral slide, the basketball hoop posts wrapped in foam to keep the children from harm should they run into them.

Behind the playground, the proposed fracking site sits dark under starlight and gilded crescent moon. There are no fences or gates surrounding it. A single bulldozer sits lonely on the empty lot. She is a little afraid, but her backbone, sturdy and expansive, a tree trunk of mud and twigs, ice and granite, has widened with new rings. The machine's cap opens just as the website said it would, and she pours both gallons of bleach into the oil reservoir.

Sister does not know whether her efforts will ultimately change anything at all, but for this moment, her joints have stopped aching. When the pain returns, suddenly, she closes her eyes. She imagines her doubt and her fear encapsulated by her pain. She imagines holding all of it in the palm of her hand, white-hot, imagines placing it humbly on an altar.

Please accept this offering, she prays. Turns out she can't, after all these years, give God the silent treatment. She believes that He has seen her, that He always sees her, even when He doesn't respond.

Sister returns to the candle glow of the vestibule off the main sanctuary. She does not know whether to expect a blessing or a punishment. The silence sits still in the chapel air, breaks into particulates, clings like incense smoke. At dawn, there is a mini-Mardi Gras moment when sunlight streams through the stained-glass windows and lights the hard wooden pews with flecks of purple, gold, green. This beauty is neither miracle nor God's voice. Sister sees this beauty every day, like the sunrise, no matter how she behaves.

SISTER WALKS TO THE house she grew up in, a few blocks away, where Ruth and Mano live together. It is late May. The dogwood trees along the sidewalk tremble in brilliant, full pastel bloom. The early tulips are stripped and spent, but the late-bloomers are opening in yellows and purples—Easter colors, come months too late. The morning sky is opening, brightening into blue. A few wispy cirrus clouds drift at high altitude, moving slowly away from the Rocky Mountain range in the west.

Sister arrives to find Ruth and Mano asleep in the living room, snoring drunken staccato harmonies. A jar of olives, festive in green and red, sits next to an assortment of open bottles—vodka, gin—on the kitchen table, which makes Sister remember their father's delicate way of saying that he was plenty drunk enough.

"No thanks," he'd say, waving away a fifth or sixth martini, "I'm halfway through a jar of olives already."

Sister fills the coffee percolator at the sink, the weight of the water intensifying the arthritic ache in her gnarled, swollen knuckles. She lights the burner and sits back down at the table. She smiles at her drunken, sleepy sisters, both blinking themselves awake. She doesn't worry about their drinking. It looks more like fun than sin.

Sister unpins her gray veil, lays it over the back of an empty chair.

"Look out, Mano," Ruth says, holding onto the *n* just a bit long, "Sister took off her veil. This party is about to go wild."

"Stop it, Ruth," Mano says. "Sister always follows the rules. We should encourage this sort of thing." Mano, the darling youngest, the buffer.

"What would Father Morel say?" Ruth says. She winks at Mano.

"There is no stone tablet, anywhere, with decrees about an itchy veil." Sister is working on loosening up. She can no longer discern, through contemplative prayer and meditation, the clear difference between God and the law. She thinks on this all the time.

"Hard to know if I can trust you," Ruth tells Sister, "without your veil on."

Gretchen, Ruth's great-granddaughter, walks into the room. She wears soft flannel pajamas. Her long brown hair has tangled like a rat's nest, and when she rubs her eyes with two tiny fists,

Sister can see chipped pink polish on her fingernails. Sister is happily surprised, feels her love for this child warm her body, a tidal surge of joy that lifts her aching shoulders.

"Sister's here," Gretchen says, delighted. Sister can see herself, can see Ruth and Mano, through Gretchen's eyes. She and her sisters have become soft, roly-poly. They are huggable, like giant teddy bears. They carry shortbread cookies in their sensible purses.

"Marilyn's been put on bed rest," Ruth says. Marilyn, Gretchen's mother, Ruth's granddaughter, is eight months pregnant with her second baby.

"Mommy's having a boy," Gretchen says.

"You'll have a brother," Sister says, and Gretchen smiles.

"She's going to name him Finch," Gretchen says.

"Such happy little birds," Mano says. "They bounce when they fly."

"Lovely," Sister says. She has never heard of a boy named Finch, but she's heard stranger names. "How's she doing?"

"She's strong," Ruth says. "Bored, but strong." Sister is comforted by Ruth's certainty.

Gretchen will start kindergarten at St. Paul's this year. She climbs into Sister's lap. The child is tiny, weighs almost nothing. Sister pictures hollow bird bones, feather down, pink fluttering unblemished lungs. She imagines Gretchen on the school playground, imagines the day in the coming spring when Gretchen will learn, as a warm breeze pops green leaves onto the oak trees behind her, the proper way to pump her own legs, to swing without a push, to fly. Sister pictures the gas well site behind the swing set, pictures Gretchen rising to meet the flare stack fumes. Sister does not want Gretchen to fly in frack-chemical air. Sister wants Gretchen to have a healthy brother named Finch, for Marilyn to recover her energy and her joy. Sister wants clean air, birdsong, cool water to drink.

If you don't want all these things too, Sister prays, *I'd like to know why you bothered making them at all.*

Sister has kept her bleach sabotage a secret even from Ruth and Mano. They would help her if she asked, and she has thought about asking, but there is something thrilling about operating alone. Sister wonders how much of this is her own vanity. She has gone out with her bleach twice more, but still the site is leveled and cleared, the work progresses. Someone has added a few T-posts with *Keep Out* signs attached, but Sister has heard nothing about her attempts at sabotage, not in the news, not from the parishioners she sees every day. It takes so much energy to misbehave, more now that it appears to have had no effect.

Sister carries a copy of the recent letter from the Vatican stating the priests' concerns that nuns across the United States are facilitating sin. The nuns, the priests worry, have become radical feminists rather than Catholics. Father Morel is a signatory of the letter. There are nuns, some whom Sister knows well, in prison for protesting the Republican National Convention, nuns in prison by their own choice, to minister to other inmates. None of these nuns were suspended from their orders for their justice protests, but none of these nuns protested during the time of the Vatican's investigation. Sister does not want to go to prison, does not want to be suspended from the order, but something in her feels enclosed now, separate, called to act up. Sister wants to believe this is God unsettling her. In the silence, she has no certainty about this.

"The parish meeting is tomorrow," Mano says. "Save us the good seats, won't you?"

SISTER MAKES COFFEE IN preparation for the meeting, aggressively rinses mugs that have collected dust in the cabinets.

She watches the room fill through the large window above the serving counter that separates the kitchen from the fellowship hall. John March, the owner of the oil field service contractor that will lead the drilling, stands next to Tommy Prince, the mayor, both fumbling with manila folders, laptops. John March seems to be watching her, has made eye contact a few times. Sister wonders what he knows, or what he suspects, and then she smiles, because no good Catholic would suspect an old lady nun of anything but upright, law-abiding behavior.

It was Ruth who untwined the viny, murderous umbilical cord from Tommy's infant neck. Ruth who once wiped the vernix, thick and clotted, from the nose and mouth of Johnny March, so that he could begin the squalling fuss through which he continues to express his unrelenting discontent with the world. The two men, best friends, were holy terrors in Sister's kindergarten classroom. She can picture them both at the art station, years ago, dipping their entire hands in the red finger paint, reaching into their shirts to make fart noises with their armpits, scaring the other students with the fake blood effect. She remembers the resigned sigh of John March's mother, the overreaction of Tommy's.

Sister pulls the drain plug from the sink. It is a large basin. This kitchen is built to feed the congregational masses. The water swirls and gurgles, the sound echoing off the wooden cupboards, each painstakingly marked with plastic strips from a label maker. Tea towels. Goblets. Spoons.

Her sisters arrive with Gretchen, who runs toward Sister, eyes bright, brown braids bouncing. They sit together in a line of folding chairs. Sister feels the slightest pull as Gretchen tugs, gently, on her veil.

"Marilyn's in the hospital," Mano says, whispering so Gretchen won't hear her.

Sister puts her hand on Ruth's arm, and for a brief moment Ruth rests her head on Sister's shoulder. "I almost didn't come," Ruth says, "I'm heading there right after."

"I want to thank you all for coming," Tommy Prince says to the room, which has become crowded and restless, uncomfortable.

Tommy Prince is handsome. He is the town's golden child. Mano leans in toward Ruth, whispers, "I wouldn't kick that one out of bed for eating crackers."

Sister giggles. Ruth rolls her eyes.

Tommy Prince continues talking. "I'm excited about so many good jobs coming here to our little town. I understand some of you have concerns, so I'm going to turn the microphone over to our own John March. I'm sure he can put your minds at ease."

Ruth leans in, whispers, "Spare me the nonsense of men lying into microphones."

Sister humpfs, loudly. People turn their heads to look at her.

"Like Tommy said," John March says, "thanks for coming. Of course, we understand your concerns about the project. There's been a lot of misinformation floating around out there. This video will show you that hydraulic fracturing is one hundred percent safe. There are no proven harmful effects on humans or on the environment."

Tommy pulls down a poorly mounted screen. John fumbles with the remote control for the projector. The technology does not work.

Mano stands up. "While we wait, why don't you explain some of this proof?"

Sister stands next to Mano. Gretchen stands next to Sister, tiny fingers warm against Sister's aching knuckles. She sees Father Morel watching her, sees frustration in the lines of his forehead. Sister knows that he sees her the same way he sees Gretchen when she squirms and fusses on the hard pews, bored by a sermon that does not speak to or for her. He wants Sister to sit still, pray silently, hope that God, in response, will change the world with His invisible hands.

What if I'm God's hands? Sister thinks.

She surprises herself with her teacher voice, its shocking volume, the authority it still carries. "Johnny, can you share with us, for example, the results of a longitudinal mixed-method study on the effects, specifically, of fracking emissions on children ages five through eleven when a drill site is only fifty yards from their outdoor play space?" Sister uses John March's childhood nickname out loud on purpose. She sees that it lands as she intended.

The crowd whispers, the moment gone suddenly electric. People do not expect nuns to know about things like longitudinal mixed-method studies. Sister is proud of her education. She has had to confess to vanity about that many times.

What if I'm not God's hands? Even as she thinks this, Sister can hear the faded nature of her doubt, the way it has quieted to a whisper even in her own prayers.

"Hey professor," Ruth whispers, "maybe tone it down a little."

Sister shakes her head, and Mano gives her an encouraging smile.

Ruth rolls her eyes. "Longitudinal mixed-method show-off," she mutters.

A young man, holding a baby, also stands. His hair is twisted into an unruly bun on the top of his head. "Do you plan to do any air-quality monitoring near the playground?" he asks.

Man Bun looks at Sister Agnes Mary. Sister does not recognize him. He must not be Catholic. This does not bother her. She smiles warmly at him, and he smiles back. The crowd, which Sister notices is full of young families, has gone rowdy.

Tommy's face is calm, but Sister can see a wet spot under the left armpit of his shirt. Sister remembers Tommy's little boy fascination with the capillary action of plants, his delight at the way blue dye stained the fringed edge of a white carnation. She wonders how she could have failed, so utterly, to instill respect for God's creation in him, in any of them. "We don't typically monitor the air—" Tommy continues.

"What we do," John says, interrupting, "is check all the equipment on a biweekly basis to make sure it's functioning correctly. We can address any problems right away. As long as we know the filters are working, you can be sure the air is within allowable levels."

"So you won't be monitoring, and you don't have any studies about how this will affect the children," Mano says. "Just to be clear."

"You tell him, Mano," Sister says.

"Yeah, Mano, you tell him," Gretchen echoes. The child turns to face Sister, goes up on tiptoes, grabs Sister's other hand as well. It is like dancing, like ring-around-the-rosy.

"Well, Sister, Mano, I appreciate your concern. But I know that you, that we all"—here John draws his hand, palm open, in front of his chest, indicating that he is one with the crowd—"want our children to be well fed and cared for. This is how we recover from the recession. These jobs are going to get our town moving in the right direction."

Sister can see that most of the crowd agrees with John, that Man Bun is an exception. Sister sees young mothers nodding, hears murmurs of support. A few people applaud. One man pumps his fist in the air and says, "Right on, John."

Man Bun begins arguing with this other citizen, and the crowd dissolves into chaos until Tommy is able to get the video projector to work. He dims the lights and sits down, looking relieved. John March stares daggers at Sister.

Ruth rushes out after the video. Other people mill about the basement, drinking coffee, eating cookies that have begun to stale.

Mano holds a sleepy Gretchen in her lap. The atmosphere calms into something like resignation. Father Morel approaches Sister.

"Mr. March is a generous parishioner," Father says. "His own children will be on that playground. You should be more respectful."

Sister's life, until recently, has been full of the fear of this sort of reprimand, but she cannot take this boy-priest seriously as a spiritual leader. She almost laughs out loud, but then she remembers herself at twenty-eight, sanctimonious, sure of all the wrong things. She has a moment of empathy. Maybe, at twenty-eight, this would have looked like leadership to her, too.

"I wiped the snot from Johnny March's nose," Sister says. "Just because he's willing to risk his own children for money doesn't mean he should get to risk everyone else's."

"The jobs in oil and gas feed these families"—Father Morel gestures for emphasis, his pointer finger raised to the sky.

Sister thinks of Marilyn, in the cold hospital room, fighting to keep her baby boy alive. "And they should have to poison them in order to feed them?"

Sister prays. *This can't possibly be your plan.*

Father Morel drops his eyes, walks away. It is as though he hadn't been speaking to her at all.

That night, Sister returns to the vestibule, prays the rosary silently except the end of every "Glory Be," which she half sings, half sobs. She thinks of the way finches bounce when they fly, such happy little birds. Her prayers echo in the empty sanctuary.

As it was in the beginning, is now and ever shall be, world without end. Amen.

EARLY JUNE BRINGS UNSEASONABLE heat. Without attention to irrigation and watering, drought parches the lawns. Finch is kept alive by NICU tubes, his prognosis unclear. The drill rig is on-site near the school playground. Ruth and Mano throw a dinner party. "Let's just try to make a little joy," Ruth says.

They curl Gretchen's hair into Shirley Temple ringlets, let her drink Hawaiian Punch and 7Up until her mouth is stained red, teach her the kick and twirl of the schottische, just as their father taught them. They wear the girl out so well that Marilyn has to carry her, sleeping, to the car.

When it is only the sisters left sitting around the table with their gin rummy, Ruth says, "I don't trust that look on your face, Sister."

"Have another drink," Sister says. "You'll trust everyone then."

"We know you're up to something," Mano says.

"You don't," Sister says.

"Sure we do," Ruth says.

Mano giggles into her tumbler. Ruth swirls her drink in circles. Sister adds a splash of vodka to her cranberry juice, hears ice cracking. Her sisters carry on, lighting thick cigars and chatting. Sister is not wearing cat-eye glasses or a corsage or her best dress from 1968 (let out a few sizes) as a gag, like the other two, but she is relaxed tonight, vaguely euphoric, grateful. She has still heard nothing about the bleach.

She leaves the house through the screen door that opens onto Ruth's back porch and stands there for a moment, taking in the evening, the joy she feels in her freedom to move through it. There is no wind. The night is crisp, the moon illuminates the pink ruffles of Ruth's peonies in the rock garden. The backyard catalpa tree she and her sisters climbed as girls has opened into a spectacular June bloom, and Sister hears owls calling back and forth in the canopy, though it seems too late in the season. She decides that it can't be wrong to want to act for this world while she's still in it.

She calls inside to her sisters, "Time for me to head home." She hefts her tote bag over her shoulder and walks into the dark night. She is through the backyard and two houses down the alley when she hears Ruth and Mano. They are shushing each other and giggling, telling each other in loud voices to quiet down. They are louder than normal, the way drunks who are trying to be quiet are always louder than normal.

They are faster than Sister and soon Mano's arm is through her right elbow, Ruth's through her left. She tries to be severe, even though part of her heart kindles when they touch her. "You two go home," she says, her voice landing somewhere between a whisper and a hiss.

The owls follow the sisters, their calls an alarm.

"Go home," Sister says again. "You'll get in trouble."

This sets Ruth and Mano into another fit of giggles.

"Hear that, Mano?" Ruth says. "Sister thinks we'll get in trouble."

"And what about you?" Mano says. "Last I checked, that's a habit, not body armor."

"Wonder Woman," Ruth says, red-faced, still laughing.

"Super-Nun," Mano says.

Sister humpfs. "You two," she begins, but they finish with her, in unison, "are really snagging my knits."

This only makes Ruth and Mano laugh louder, squeeze her more tightly between them. They have fallen into step with Sister, and the three of them move in tandem, like a marching band, on the sidewalk, on the newly greened tree lawns. They are approaching the playground now, the flare stack flame stretching toward the full moon, the chains on the swings knocking together in the chill, steady breeze.

They reach the swings and each sister takes one, sits for a moment. Ruth and Mano laugh like loons.

"Sober up," Sister says, harshly. Ruth and Mano stop laughing.

Sister reaches into her tote bag, pulls out the U-locks. Her joints ache so badly she almost loses her grip. "I'm going to lock myself to the machine."

"Then we are too," Mano says.

"Not enough locks," Sister says.

Ruth rolls her eyes and points as she counts out loud. "One, two, three. Three locks, three sisters."

Sister stands up and squares her shoulders. She tries to stretch herself to look tall. She smiles, shakes her head. "I'm going alone," she says. "I want this for myself."

"What will Father Morel say?" Ruth asks.

Sister shrugs. Ruth nods. Mano hiccups.

"I'm not supposed to want things for myself," Sister says, "but I do."

Ruth nods again. "I guess God knows you're human."

Moisture from the irrigation ditch has slicked the weeds between the playground and the drill site. The sisters stumble and slip, but they make it past the *Keep Out* signs and into the clearing. The machines there—the water tank trailers, the industrial blender—are giants. Terrifying faces form in the patterns of the mixers and meters that line the side of the blender. The injector shines in the moonlight. It takes effort to make the sign of the cross, but Sister does it twice, once over herself and once over the U-locks.

Ruth and Mano move toward her as she picks up the first lock, but Sister holds up one hand between herself and her sisters. Mano and Ruth step back.

The pain is excruciating, all-encompassing, as if her joints have split open to leak poison into the rest of her, but her soul feels once more fertile and verdant, honeysuckle over boxwood, evergreen. Sister persists, but she moves so slowly through her pain that she worries she will not finish the job before the men arrive.

"This is silly," Ruth says, grabbing the lock out of Sister's hands.

Mano and Ruth help fasten a U-lock around each of her ankles, connect her right hand to a small gauge wheel.

"Thank you," Sister says. "Now scram."

Mano gives Sister a hug. Ruth simply nods, but when they get to the edge of the clearing, both Mano and Ruth turn and wave. The sunrise looks like Gretchen's pastel hair ribbons. Sister, as she has done her whole life, prays fervently. She listens intently for a response from heaven but hears only the owls in the distance, near one another, calling back and forth.

When you called us to protect your creation, Sister prays, *this is what you meant, right?* The silence that follows is a conglomerate silence, the heavy sum of the million tiny silences that have built Sister's faith.

She sees a diesel truck heading toward her, a man behind the wheel, and she imagines this man is Johnny March, angry, dragon-like. She pictures Johnny as a wide-eyed kindergartener in need of protection. She pictures herself the same way. She imagines her feet supported by moonlight, the prick of feathers growing through the skin on her back. Sister gathers her wits. She wills herself to stay visible.

Man Camp

—

THE MAN CAMP WAS the biggest town for god knows how many North Dakota miles, built to be torn down like fucking LEGOs when the Bakken ran dry and the whole thing busted, which everyone knew it would. The bust was a sure thing, but the timing was anyone's guess, and guessing was everyone's favorite topic. Joe knew exactly as much about the oil field as he needed to do his job, which wasn't much, but he joined in with his own loud predictions, debated whether the proper unit was months, years, decades. He was doing it now, this morning, over strong coffee and crisp cafeteria bacon, until Dustin called bullshit.

"Dude. Put the crystal ball away already," he said, his mouth full of Froot Loops from the self-serve cereal hopper. "You don't know and it don't matter. We work until the work runs out. Then we can fear the reaper."

Joe pictured Will Ferrell and a cowbell, wondered if this was a reference he and Dustin shared. Dustin was barely twenty-one, fresh out of his parents' house, the biggest disappointment of his life so far an unsuccessful search for a steady girlfriend. Every break he got, Dustin went home to his mother's chili and cinnamon rolls, to beers with his high school buddies.

"You mean face the reaper. At the end, you face him."

In the cafeteria, Dustin flashed a smile, revealing the benefits of teenage orthodontics. "What I mean, Joe, is YOLO."

"Yoyo?" Joe was messing with him now. He knew what YOLO meant, felt the oppressive truth of YOLO like spiders crawling on his skin.

Dustin's hair stuck up at odd angles, and Joe fought an urge to pat the kid on the head, make him look more presentable. Through the thin plastic wall that separated their bedrooms, the kid sounded like a sixty-year-old man. Dustin's smoker's hack, exacerbated by a nasty bronchitis he'd picked up somewhere, had woken Joe multiple times. Joe found himself stealing the kid's cigarettes, tossing them into trash cans at random gas stations. It was how he would have handled it with his own son, if his own son had grown up to be a smoker, but DJ hadn't gotten the chance to grow up at all. Joe felt his hands burn and tingle, then, and before the feeling could spread to his chest, to the raw mess of his heart, he closed his eyes, willed himself to stop thinking about it. It was like closing a set of blinds to hide a wildfire blazing outside the window. Temporary relief, false, but relief all the same.

Joe had been in the man camp for about a year, and he had to admit it lived up to the promises of the recruiter he had spoken to back in Colorado, who had sold a comfortable life (*Amenities like you wouldn't believe! Better than home! Hassle-free!*) and the chance to make his fortune driving water trucks for the rigs. It was Joe's nature to doubt all salesmen, but in spite of his low expectations about this part of his compensation package, it was an improvement over his first gig back in Colorado. Room and board had been free there, too, a giant double-wide provided by the company stuffed with eleven other guys, bunk beds lined up like army barracks, slopped Stagg chili and Dorito powder in the shared kitchen, the smell of burnt coffee and weed and the never-ending trash can overflow, their sense of decency dropping off the same cliff as their privacy.

Joe hadn't been back to Greeley since he'd left, had decided to avoid location-based triggers that might evoke memory—his lovely wife, pregnant, laughing as a thick milkshake mustache dripped down her chin at JB's Drive In. "Say it five times fast!" Mandy had insisted, and they'd both tried it, giggling like fools, over and over. *Marshmallow milkshake mustache marshmallow milkshake mustache marshmallow milkshake mustache.* Or years later, at the junkyard off Highway 34, the one with the observation tower he'd paid a buck to climb with DJ so the boy could marvel at the view of the Rockies on the western horizon. Mandy's minivan, the car he had spent so many days off working on, had been hauled there after the wreck, was there still, he imagined, crumpled, rusting in the cruel sun. She'd driven off a bridge into the South Platte River. Witnesses reported a sudden jerky swerve, a loss of control, enough momentum to half break, half jump the crumbling concrete barrier, but there had been no sightings of what, if anything, had been blocking the road. They'd managed to pull an unconscious Mandy out in time, but DJ was already gone.

Joe asked for extra shifts instead of weeks off, and his supervisor was more than happy to shave his breaks. He killed the rare empty day playing Gran Turismo on an ancient PlayStation 2, taking breaks on the smokers' plaza. The gas rigs were a new world—unceasing, unstoppable—and working eighty, ninety hours each week had made him the small fortune he needed to pay for Mandy's care in a long-term care facility back in Greeley, where she lived now.

"We're not sure she'll ever fully recover," the nurses had told him, and he'd nodded, mute. Of course she wouldn't, and neither would he. He loved her, still he loved her, imagined her with him on the rig, an angel on his shoulder. The things he couldn't forgive he just had to bear, but Mandy was an exception—he could neither forgive her nor bear seeing her. He'd broken his own heart and left town, the condition of Mandy's heart in the capable hands of the facility staff.

Dustin stuffed his pockets with sausage biscuits and filled his thermos with coffee. Joe grabbed sack lunches for them both. "You look like shit," Joe said. "Sure you don't need a day?"

Dustin shrugged. "The cough is a real bitch at night, but it gets better in the daytime."

Joe nodded. It was the same with his dreams. In the bright light of day he didn't imagine DJ's fading struggle against his seat belt, the river current flowing through his hair, through his lungs. In the bright light of day, he didn't stop to wonder whether Mandy had a real accident or whether she'd meant to drive into that river.

WINDBLOWN GRIT SCOURED HIS face and tapped against the buildings, which bowed slightly in the heaviest gusts. Joe was happy for the long shift ahead of him, happy to be free from his dreams. Gravel crunched under his boots, louder for the 5 a.m. silence around him. The men seemed quieter at night, presumably due to the human habits of their lives before the camp, but there were always men coming in and men heading out, a twenty-four-hour stream of going to work and getting off work, sleeping and waking, being indoors and being outdoors. Even now there were guys watching *The Godfather* in the rec room, guys lifting weights in the fitness area, guys walking to the bunks, hoods pulled over their heads to shield them from the relentless prairie wind. The lens coating on his sunglasses was scraped and scratched nearly off from the grit that pelted him as he worked.

He and Dustin were set to ride together, and once Joe got the kid talking his own mind could drift away on the conversational current—he could nod, hum a few times, offer occasional low-stakes advice on Dustin's low-stakes twenty-one-year-old life, call it a day well lived. At the truck, Dustin paused. "Give me a minute, will you? I forgot I need new laces."

Joe shrugged. The kid was lucky the camp store was open this early. The store didn't carry much—boot laces, work gloves, cigarettes, Twinkies. Joe sat on the back bumper and looked at the sky. The camp lights were no match for the bright splashes of starlight—Joe had never before been able to see the distant sparkle of the cosmos so clearly. There had always been too much light right in front of him, light that tethered him to the moment. His mind wandered up and into the expanse, so that when the man approached, Joe startled.

The man smiled, held out his hand. "Ben Stone. Company recruiter. You're Joe Baker?"

Stone was a grizzled old guy, mid-seventies maybe, a paper copy of the *Tribune* under one arm and a set of pencils, actual lead pencils, the kind that needed to be sharpened in one of those rotary sharpeners from grade school, in the front pocket of his shirt. A little old for the rigs themselves, Stone had arrived a week ago for a site visit. Dustin had heard he was retired from some high school in Bismarck, a history teacher, and he looked the part.

Joe shook Stone's hand. "Good to meet you." Joe cleared his throat to shake the sleep from his voice. "You out from Bismarck?"

"Yep. Turned me loose into the field for a few days. I have to say, I was expecting worse. The food is really quite good, though I would never tell my wife that. Quieter than I thought it would be—I pictured it like something from a Steinbeck novel. Not quite *Grapes of Wrath* because, no family, you know? But maybe *Cannery Row*."

Joe laughed. Steinbeck was the only author he'd actually liked in high school English. "Not near enough alcohol for that. Too many rules."

"It's some kind of frog hunting, I guess." Stone shrugged. "I've seen your file. Community college. Associate's but no bachelor's. Former land surveyor. How'd you end up here?"

Joe never knew how much to share. He thought of Mandy as he'd last seen her, in a wheelchair in the assisted living recreation room, a blanket on her lap, her hair greasy and stringy, staring out the window at the red pop of house finches against the spruce outside. Her eyes neutral until she saw him, then a speechless glare that drilled him with hate, with blame. Her silent accusations had reacted with the secret doubts he kept buried, and one thing he knew for sure—Mandy's depression had eaten at the heart of their family life for years, and he, for all those years, had been resentful instead of compassionate. "Turns out hauling water pays better than surveys, at least once the recession hit. I needed the money."

"You still have family back in Colorado?"

How much of his life were people prepared to take in response to such pleasantries? "My wife is in assisted living. She doesn't really . . . she has a brain injury."

"I'm sorry to hear that." Stone had what Mandy would have called kind eyes, and Joe was surprised by the older man's sincerity, and then was surprised by his surprise, by how long it had been since he had believed in anyone else's honesty.

"Here's the thing, Joe. We need an advance land guy back there in Weld County. Someone to secure easements from property owners, convince them to allow us to get the seismic testing done, reassure them that they won't start being able to light their water faucets on fire. Company likes to promote from within, we need someone who knows the area, and you seem to stand right out. You interested?"

Joe let out a low whistle. "When do you need to know?"

"Soon." Stone smiled. "You could do a lot worse than this, you know."

He knew. He nodded, watched Stone pass Dustin as the kid rushed toward the truck, boots unlaced, shrugging into an insulated work jacket. He let the prairie wind rage against his skin until his nose ran, until tears pooled in the corner of his eyes.

"Hey! You met the guy. Who is he?" Dustin was breathless from rushing.

"Recruiter." Joe pictured Stone in a solid brick library surrounded by century-old oak trees, reading *East of Eden*. How did a guy like that end up in the oil field, still wearing a jacket with leather-patched elbows? It didn't make sense.

"He offer you something good? Something closer to home?" Dustin rubbed his jaw like he'd taken a hard punch. "Take me with you, man. I have to get back there. My girl is not into this long-distance thing."

Joe shook his head. "I'd been married for two years by the time I was your age." Mandy was barely marriage legal, but after a whirlwind month of dating she had filled up all his empty spaces. He'd never felt so full of anything. He wondered what the justice of the peace must have thought—impulsive teenage lovers, reckless, broke. Mandy had worn a purple satin dress from her senior prom, braided ditch sunflowers into her hair, slipped her shoes off in the courthouse hallway.

"Married? Where's your ring?"

Joe rubbed his ring finger with his thumb. "Too much it could catch on up here."

"How come you never go home then? Come on, Joe. We been working together for too long for you not to have mentioned a wife."

"A wife and a son. She had an accident, needs assisted living back in Greeley. My boy didn't make it."

Dustin gasped. The kid's eyes were welling, and Joe was struck by the gesture, Dustin's emotions laid bare between them, as though there was nothing to fear in turning them loose. Emotion did not reconcile easily with life in the man camp. Dustin was just like he'd been at that age, so full of cocky absolute certainty that the way he lived or ate or thought was the one right way to do any of those things. Dustin hadn't lived long enough to fuck it all up, to fail at important things. He couldn't realize how much of life was the luck, good or bad, that flowed out of the crap choices you made before the stakes were clear, before you knew how to properly care for the things you held dear.

In Joe's dreams, memory held hands with the imaginary, inter-twined like fingers, and a withered, ghost-like Mandy pointed at him, scowling, so accusatory, so suddenly lucid, and then it was Joe, not Mandy, who had driven the Caravan off the bridge, and he was frozen, unable to flee, guilt shining from his skin in visible rays. Sometimes it was DJ, all curls and bounce and innocence, scrambling around the riverbank rocks, asking incessantly if Joe wanted to try a different fly, and Joe felt ashamed of the annoyance he had felt toward his son in that past moment, regret flooding his present-day self. Sometimes a twisted gas rig leaked poison into a burning river, and it was Joe's own limp, lifeless body, not DJ's, trapped under the currents.

"How old was he, your son?" Dustin had wiped his eyes, the moment hardening between them.

Joe shook his head. It was already too much. He hadn't talked about it to anyone at the man camp, and nobody had asked. Part of what made it work, all that lonely, was an unspoken prohibition against curiosity. The men didn't pick at each other's scabs. "Time to roll, kid."

"It's like that, eh?" Dustin shrugged. "All right, Joe. I'm always just waiting on you."

THE SHIFT WENT BY. The drilling rig had left the site the week before, and the injector, after a minor repair, was put back to work. There was a bit of tension with the flare until it was clear that all was working the way it should. Dustin was a sloppy worker—leaving tools at various job sites, half-assing the cleanup, half-assing most things. He cut corners. Today, it was a connection to the water tank that leaked gallons before Joe caught it, prairie dirt becoming prairie mud all over the men's boots.

Joe caught Dustin by the jacket sleeve. "You got to take some pride in what you do."

"Pride," Dustin laughed, shaking his head like it was some kind of joke, but Joe noticed that he doubled back, tightened things up, that the work he did the rest of the day was focused, beyond reproach.

He thought about Stone's offer, and suddenly he wanted more than anything to unlock the unlikely chimes of Mandy's laughter, see her smile at the cheerful tittering of house finches, the smell of spruce through the open window. Rig life and marriage were the same. During boom times, everyone made bets about when the bust would happen, and during the bust, it was hard to believe there would ever be another boom. He wished he could scare his past self into the moment, like Marley to Scrooge, make his past self kinder in the face of Mandy's sinking sadness. Joe as the ghost of his own empty future. Joe lost.

Joe forced himself to give the job his attention. *I'll get just as sloppy as Dustin.* All of the site activity was hidden from view by giant water tanks. It was an unspoken rule that the rigs should be hidden as much as possible—not, of course, that the company had anything to hide. In this case, Joe wondered whose view they were worrying about, as this particular site was so remote they hadn't seen any sign of humanity since they turned off the state highway miles back. The truck convoys hauling water were one of the most visible things for local people to object to . . . so much traffic on once-sleepy rural roads. But he knew it would be worse if the entire drilling process was so tangible. What the public could see, the flare burning off the emissions, the giant drill rig, the twenty-four-hour spotlights, was upsetting enough, but the invisible turmoil underneath it all—underground explosives, chemical soup, toxic gases— was far more frightening.

His mother's face had been that same kind of façade—a mask of false serenity, her anger at being left to raise Joe alone always simmering somewhere beneath it. He'd realized too late, after he left home too, how heartbreakingly lonely the eerie calm of the house must have been for her. He remembered himself, a frightened ten-year-old, asking her about the erections he had started getting on a regular basis. During math class. On the school bus. Riding his bike. His father years gone by then, he'd had no one else to ask.

"What's happening? Am I okay?" His mother had been scrubbing dishes with a sour-smelling sponge. Her yellow rubber-gloved hand had slowed only for a moment, her grip almost imperceptibly tightening.

"Of course you're okay," she had said, refusing eye contact. "Just don't think about it and it will go away."

Joe returned to that advice over and over again, a simple truth around which he organized his life. It was what had drawn him to trade the plains of Colorado for the North Dakota prairie, to ignore completely the earnest urgings of the social worker at Mandy's facility to "re-engage with society." He was working to master his thoughts, to disengage from complex moral conflict. This job was the only luck he'd had in the past few years. He knew the company had saved his ass, saved the asses of any number of other men who had been laid off from jobs in construction, in landscaping, in mortgage lending, for God's sake, during the recession. He didn't want to dwell on the environmental impacts, the political bickering, and certainly not on Mandy, or on DJ.

And then the shift was over and he and Dustin were back in the truck, the empty Dakota road spread out ahead of them, surrounded by prairie. Rough-legged hawks perched on the ranch fence posts, stark against the open country. At thirty-eight, Joe often felt like an old man, in camp and on-site, surrounded by green, disillusioned millennial boys who'd believed they'd make their fortunes as pro football stars or white rappers, who'd paid just enough attention in high school to graduate. They'd leveraged those diplomas into jobs on the rigs with training and good pay—pay that, for the most part, the young guys took for granted, felt they somehow deserved. Dustin was different from most in that he could see beyond the moment. Dustin's plan, Joe knew, was a degree in alternative energy from the community college, a future entrepreneur masquerading as an oil patch roughneck.

"Maybe something like, we can't even imagine now, you know?" Dustin was a talker. "Like in *Back to the Future*, when Doc stuffs garbage into his DeLorean to make gas. That's what I'm doing in my thirties, man. Stacks of bills. No more of this raping the earth and shit."

"You've got vision," Joe said, surprised by his own sincerity, by how invested he was starting to feel in Dustin's success. "That'll take you far. That and saving. You're making plenty of money up here for community college."

"Okay, Dad," Dustin said, joking, and then the color drained from his face. "Nah, man, I'm sorry. I wasn't thinking about your . . . I wasn't thinking."

Joe shrugged it off. He was old enough to have helped his mother, a legal secretary, lug a typewriter home so she could work nights. He'd used clunky DOS desktops in high school, had bought a laptop for the business that had failed, and now, as water hauler, somehow all he needed was a pocket-sized phone. When the drilling was done and this whole thing busted, maybe he'd find himself begging a millionaire Dustin for a job. The world got harder to recognize the longer he lived in it, and only sometimes did that have to do, directly, with the loss of DJ.

"All I meant, dude," Dustin said, "is that I don't necessarily want to be like you when I'm your age. Fifteen years, for me? I'm gonna have a family, my own business, a fucking BMW. I'm going to work clean. No more dirt and shit all over my clothes." Joe felt gut-punched, humiliated. Still, he hoped he would see Dustin do better than he'd done for himself, even if it shamed his own life some. Maybe it wasn't his place to feel that for Dustin. Then again, maybe Dustin was a fine place for all his feelings to land. *Okay, Dad.*

THEY PULLED INTO THE man camp, exhausted. Dustin had picked up Joe's habit of ladling soup into a mug, drinking it on the walk from the cafeteria to the bunk, collapsing into as much sleep as possible before they were back to switching tanks in the wind-howl and the swirling dust devils. Today, Joe sat for a few minutes, ate his mac and cheese with a real fork. He pulled up CNN to check the headlines but got distracted by sponsored links and ended up on YouTube, watching something called a Whizbang chicken plucker a farmer had built out of an old washing machine. The farmer fired up the motor, shot a garden hose into the basket, and dropped in a beheaded, bled-out bird. Feathers and water splashed into the air for a minute, and the bird emerged totally bare, like a rubber chicken from an old slapstick gag. The farmer, all enthusiasm, raved about the speed and quality of the pluck. Joe almost laughed out loud.

It was then he noticed Stone, a few tables over, working on a crossword, brow furrowed. When Joe sat down across from him, Stone seemed exasperated. "Any guesses about a suffix suggesting noodles?"

The metal eraser casing of each of the pencils poking out of the top of Stone's shirt pocket was empty and bent. An old Stetson sat on the table next to him. Joe wondered why Stone, who seemed to have been cultivating this cowboy professor look for years, neglected to use a pocket protector. The bottom seam of his shirt pocket was marked and stained with lead. "Try -*aroni*?"

Stone paused, then attacked the page with a gum eraser. "Right," he said, "but that means these two down answers can't be right. Anyway, you got an answer for me?"

Joe felt his hands start to shake, hid them in his jacket pocket. "I could use some details about the offer."

Stone put the paper down. His eyebrows, gray, bushy caterpillars, crawled toward his hairline. "Significant salary increase, with bonuses. Stock options. Nice private office in our Greeley headquarters. I hear it's got a mountain view and everything. Company truck. Relocation paid, though looking at the, well, simplicity of your situation here, we may be able to swap out the moving expenses for a down payment toward a house. You keep your benefits."

"When would I start?"

"Two weeks to get yourself settled down there, and then you're on the job."

Memories appeared at the worst times. Here was DJ stumbling on the rocks on a foothills hike, red dirt scuffed into shoes that flashed neon lights when he stepped on them. DJ on the top of a rock he'd labored to climb, his arms spread wide, spinning slowly, the joy of accomplishment streaming from somewhere near his tiny boy heart, ribboning into the big sky, combining, in the end, with the placid cumulus clouds above. Here were the ways Mandy's joy had morphed into brooding darkness, her maddening silences broken only by the blare of the TV. Here was the flare and release of his own anger as he grabbed her shoulders and yelled, "Pull it together, Mandy. Jesus. Do something. Do anything. If you can't be happy with this, make a fucking change."

Joe could almost picture Mandy's eyes rolling, then boring straight into him, each one its own kind of drill rig. He could almost hear her laugh out loud, as though she were with him in the man camp cafeteria, saying, *That's right, jackass. Not so easy to take your own advice, is it?*

Joe tried to swallow the lump out of his throat. He appreciated Stone's patience. The man just sat there as Joe struggled to pull himself together. "Can I sleep on it?"

Stone nodded, went back to his crossword puzzle.

BACK AT HIS BUNK, Joe used the Jack-and-Jill bathroom he and Dustin shared. Drifting into sleep, he wondered how many of the other guys knew that term, a Jack-and-Jill bathroom, from their lives at home with their wives or girlfriends. He wondered if knowing it made them as lonely as it made him. He woke to a film of dust and tears crusting his eyes nearly shut, and when he cleaned his ears after his shower, the swab came out blackened and greasy. The bunks were small, a single bed, a closet with drawers inside, a small counter/desk with a mirror above it, something Mandy would have called a vanity. In the middle, there was just enough space for one man to stand up. Visitors were naturally discouraged by the tightness of the space. Women, drugs, and alcohol weren't allowed in the rooms at all.

Joe went outside into the afterglow of a spent sunset. The evening was calm, the wind settled. Dustin sat in a plastic deck chair nursing a bottle of chocolate milk, texting. He didn't look up when Joe sat down, his fingers nearly blurring across the touch screen of his phone. Joe hated the kid's distractibility, the assumption that the human in front of you, face-to-face, should wait in favor of the human on the other end of the digital world.

"I think someone was in my room when we were gone," Dustin said. "It just looked . . . I don't know, like someone was in there."

"Spot inspection, probably," Joe said. "You didn't have any contraband, did you?" After the mess of the trailer in Greeley, Joe was grateful to have his own room, understood that he had traded privacy for convenience here in the camp. He accepted it as a condition of employment.

"They got no right to go through my room. It's in like . . . the Constitution or some shit."

Joe shrugged. "It's in your contract. Besides, it's not like your parents never searched your room, lurked on your Facebook, read your texts. You're too young for privacy."

Dustin's jaw dropped. Joe could almost see him searching his memories for examples of this exact kind of injustice. "That's fucked up, man. I mean, I thought I lost a dime bag once, but maybe my dad just took it and didn't have the balls to say anything, you know?" The kid, betrayed, looked even younger than normal.

Joe felt like such an ass, sowing the seeds of discontent between this kid and what was probably his perfectly well-meaning, loving father. It was exactly this contrariness, this need to point out flaws to others, that had driven Mandy crazy. "Like your mother," she had said. "Just like her. Knock it off, will you?" And he had tried, he had, was still trying, really, but he never saw it until after the fact, when the razor-sharp effect of his bullshit had hit the people around him. When the wound was already inflicted, and he had no idea how to stop the bleeding.

"Stone wants to make me a land man back in Greeley." Joe needed to talk to someone, and Dustin, unbelievably, had become the only person in the world who'd listen.

"That's where your wife is, right? And it's money?" Dustin shrugged. "I guess I don't know why it's even a question."

"She might not want me," Joe said. He felt the truth of it press his shoulders toward the prairie ground, as though the man camp would absorb him easily, hide everything that terrified him, hide the ways he himself was terrifying. "She might be better off."

Dustin was back to tapping on his phone screen, no eye contact. "Sounds like you don't know for sure what she wants."

Joe used the toe of his boot to trace a line in the dust in front of his chair. He closed his eyes, leaned back against the trailer wall, and was surprised to find not a memory but a possible future. Mandy and Dustin and Joe together at JB's Drive In, the three of them laughing over milkshakes. Joe saying to Dustin, *You're lucky she likes you*, and Dustin throwing up both hands, *Of course she likes me, I'm charming as hell*, and Mandy laughing, taking Joe's hand. Nobody resurrected, everybody still alive, broken, together.

"If I had it to do over again," Joe said, "I'd do it different."

Dustin cleared his throat. "My girl down there says I'm wasting time doing this. Like I should come home and just get on with it already. Maybe she's right about that for both of us."

Joe looked out into the distance, searching for the line where land met sky. "There might be a way I can convince Stone to let you come with me. Tell him we make a good team. Batman and Robin or something."

Dustin shook his head. "I like you just fine, Joe, but I'm nobody's Robin. Still, I'd appreciate a good word, if it gets me back home."

He got out his own phone and offered it to Dustin. "You ever heard of a Whizbang chicken plucker? Maybe that's how you can make your millions. Impress this girl."

Dustin laughed, delighted, as feathers flew on the phone screen. "Funny, jackass."

JOE WATCHED THE LIGHT fade, the stars appear and twinkle. He'd find Stone in the morning, start making the arrangements. He pictured Mandy next to an open window, a cacophony of colorful birds in the burr oaks and spruce. Mandy's smile deep in her brown eyes. Mandy angelic, the sunset streaking beams of light around her. He'd grab what luck was offering here, ride it as far into the future as possible, hope his life held strong against the pressure.

Flood Stories

—

IN 1976, WHEN THE Big Thompson River swelled with monsoon rain and flooded the canyon, my mother, Beth, carried me to safety, climbing first up a steep mountain slope and then into a giant ponderosa pine, despite the way her mud-heavy shoes lost purchase on the rain-slick bark, despite the pitch on her fingers and in her hair. I was one year old, wrapped in a hand-stitched baby quilt she tied around herself as a sling. I squalled all night. The storm clouds obscured the moon, the night was black save for lightning, which, in its flashing, lit the churning river and the debris—some empty cars, some full of bodies, propane tanks, punctured, hissing fumes, trees as thick as the one we were perched in. Each flash of lightning revealed some new scene of horror, one Mom could see but I couldn't, and still I was the one who was crying. Mom has told this story, again and again, to me or in front of me, all of my life. "You never were easy to settle," she says. "Nothing I did ever contented you, not even saving your life."

Yesterday, when I told her about the job I'd been offered at the

state Parks and Wildlife office in Denver, full benefits, my own
office, twice my current salary, she added, "Nothing contents you
now, either." Then she took her cocktail glass and her cigarette out
to the porch and sat there while the sun set, a worn blanket draped
across her shrinking frame, her thinning hair a halo of static electricity. Mom is only sixty-five, but she is shrinking into herself, her
heart congested, failing. She is aging fast and angry. I think all the
time about the things I know but Mom doesn't, that I have a baby
growing in my womb, a girl, I am nearly certain, her father a one-
night stand I couldn't possibly locate now. That if I want that job,
any job better than the one I have now, manning the entry station
to Rocky Mountain National Park, I have to take it before I start
to show. I think about the things we both know but won't say out
loud. That this canyon she half raised me in has nothing that either
of us needs: no doctors, no jobs. That she should lay off the cigarettes and gin, go for more walks, eat more kale. I should do all
these things too, though I don't smoke the way she does anyhow.
Medical instructions for the end of life and the beginning of it are
surprisingly similar.

I poured a glass of cranberry juice, no vodka, and sat next to
her on the porch. I'd been living for years in this cabin along the Big
Thompson River. My grandfather rebuilt it after the '76 flood, and I
moved in after college. When Mom retired, last year, she moved in
with me, which feels similar to childhood, but harder to bear after
years of adult living.

"Come on, Mom," I said. "We could have a fine time in Denver. All that art. Poetry readings. Street festivals." *Hospitals. First
responders.*

"You're not a city kid, Lottie. You'd miss these mountains too
much."

"I'm thirty-two, Mom. I'm not any kind of kid. We need the
city and the money right now." I will miss this cabin, which feels

like mine even though we share it, though it's Mom's name on the property deed. She's right about that much. The river runs fast and high enough with the June rise to block the noise of the highway that runs on the other side of it. The rock wall of the canyon against the road turns pink-golden in the waning hours of the day, the tops of pines that line the steep mountain incline on our side of the river catch the sunset light and burn like torches. Each night, the cabin grows dark with the canyon bottom, though the sun's waning light shines in the sky above us. The tree that saved both our lives still flourishes on the steep slope nearby. Dad hated this cabin, or so Mom says, which is why he and my brother Andy weren't here the night of the flood. The fact that Dad hated the cabin makes Mom love it more, I think, out of spite.

Between us was Mom's stack of books, a few heady sociopolitical nonfiction titles, Annie Proulx, Larry McMurtry. She'd been a librarian in Loveland for forty years. Mom named me Charlotte because she loves the Brontës, loves everything dark and gothic. She'd wanted to name Andy Heathcliff but Dad put his foot down, I guess. She's locally famous for the passionate one-woman pro-beet sugar, anti-chemical sweetener campaign she ran from behind her library desk through the eighties and beyond. Mom would stamp due dates on copies of *Hop on Pop*, on *Hatchet*, on *Farmer Boy* and say to the children, or their mothers, or whoever would listen, "You can't believe the commercials. Just because it's all NutraSweet all the time doesn't mean it's actually healthy for you. Causes cancer, the doctors say, and it's putting the mill under besides."

Mom is proud of her reputation as a tough old bird, an upstanding citizen. I know it because she says it out loud. It was her most adamant lesson for Andy and me: guard your reputations, cultivate the goodwill and admiration of others, use this as currency for any number of favors, a rich array of possible rewards. Mom is at least as proud of her reputation as she is of me, I'm sure of it.

"Can you drive me to Walgreens this weekend?" Mom's doctors have advised against her getting behind the wheel. "My prescriptions will be ready on Friday."

"I'll just stop on my way home from work."

"I'd rather come with you."

"Yeah, but then I have to drive all the way here to get you, and then all the way back." Mom has this thing now where she browses. She reads greeting cards she doesn't plan to buy. She considers the sizes and shapes of Tupperware containers that won't fit in our full-to-bursting cabinets. She tests outrageous lipstick colors on her wrist. It's like entering a drugstore black hole, time itself suspended.

Mom pursed her lips and nodded. She didn't say anything else, but I know she's not letting it go, either. I picture Mom adding a stone to the disappointing daughter jar she carries in her heart. Mom keeps track, and if I'm honest, I do too, my grudges like magnets. The more I carry, the more I collect.

The wind set the tops of the trees swaying, but where we were, below, it was gentle, soft against the skin, scented with pine pitch and river water.

"In Denver there are Walgreens everywhere. Maybe even walking distance," I said.

"What makes you think I'm coming with you?" she asked.

"If I go," I said, "you can't stay up here alone."

"Like hell I can't."

She's wrong about that, in denial about her ever-shrinking independence, just like she's wrong that nothing contents me. Living with Mom in the canyon would be perfectly fine except that I can't seem to be a grown-up with her around. Every time I think I'm acting responsibly, Mom makes me feel like I'm chasing the river mist. She's wrong about who I am, but so confidently that I get to doubting myself. What she will say when she finds out I am knocked up by a stranger, I don't know. I feel like I've lost an old fight with her. I imagine her nodding, unsurprised, saying, *I always told you that's who you were.*

"I'm turning in," she said.

"It's barely dark."

"Doctors say rest. I'm resting." Mom's voice had an edge. She's especially irritable since the diagnosis. Irritability is not a symptom of congestive heart failure. I looked it up. I guess I wanted to confirm that she could help it, if she wanted to, all her special meanness.

"You feeling well enough to hike in the morning?"

"Doctors say exercise," Mom said, rubbing her swollen ankles. "They say rest, and they say exercise. The hell."

I stayed on the porch after Mom went to bed, watched the sky above the canyon fade to black, the stars begin their shimmer. When I was pretty sure she was asleep, I got my computer, which I still plug into the phone modem here in the canyon. My brother, Andy, a former cop, is in state prison. He was convicted of falsifying evidence in a number of local cases down in Loveland, lying under oath. For a while, before he got caught, Andy was the big man on the force, the go-to, the crack investigator who always got the bad guy. Mom was so proud of him, her reputation elevated by his. Andy still denies the charges, claims innocence, but I'm pretty sure he did it. The danger of investing in reputation alone is that it's easy to put it above a sense of ethics. Andy wanted to be the best crime-stopper so badly that he started to invent criminals to stop, didn't see until it was too late the way that made him a criminal himself. I don't condone the choices he made, but I understand them.

Mom took Andy's side, the last person to recognize that he really had gone crooked, even as the evidence stacked up. Bobby Jackson wasn't cooking meth at the old sugar mill. Sally James did not embezzle any funds from the United Way. I try to give Mom credit for doing the right thing eventually, calling Andy out, but her sudden shift seemed cowardly to me, a move made solely to protect her own reputation from the downfall of his. The worst part of all of it is that Andy's wife, Leah, has to raise their little boy on her own now. She lets Mom and me take Tyler to McDonald's every so often, but she can't forgive us any more than she can forgive Andy. Mom gets indignant about that, but I don't blame Leah one bit.

I pay the fees required for me and Andy to send emails back and forth, or at least, for me to send him emails. I write about the doctor's visits and the prognosis, about Mom's dry cough and how much weight she's lost. He almost never responds. A few days ago, I wrote about myself, about the pregnancy, and when I pulled up the system, he'd gotten back to me.

Wish I could be a fly on the wall when you tell Mom.

I closed my laptop, buried my face in my hands. Andy never cared much about feelings. Not mine. Not anyone's. "This is tough love," he'd say, his face heavy, emotionless. "You'll thank me someday," but I don't. Life is hard enough without everyone you love trying to harden you further. When my baby is born, I'll be all marshmallow. Feather down. Fleece. I'll be the softest thing my baby touches, the softest thing that touches her.

I HAVE A FLOOD story about Mom, too, a different one, but I don't tell it to anyone but myself. When Dad left us in January of 1990, it hit me differently than it hit Mom, in that I felt, generally, that I was better off without him, a feeling I've managed to project onto the men I've dated since, none of whom have stuck around long. Mom kept food in the fridge, drove us to school, put on a brave face at the library. Everyone admired her strength in adversity, but at home she stared out windows, absent, her body with us but her mind gone cumulus. I turned fifteen that year, on Valentine's Day, a few days before the giant molasses tank in the Great Western yard ruptured, sent a knee-deep flow of molasses, glacial and viscous, across Madison Avenue, which was much less glamorous than it sounds, the bankrupt sugar mill on one side of the street, a well-kept little trailer park on the other.

I will admit that my memories from childhood, even those teen years, are shady at best, but I do think the moments I remember at all are the moments that built me. One early teenage Easter, I wore the dress I'd worn the year before, because there was no money for a new one. When I came downstairs, my father choked on the beer he'd taken to drinking with breakfast, and said to Mom, not to me, "She's not going to church looking like some sort of whore," and then he stormed out to the lawn chair he kept on the front porch. Dad got laid off from the sugar mill the same time everyone else did. He had been distant before, easily irritated, but the layoff turned him mean.

I pulled at the seam of my skirt, trying to stretch it past mid-thigh. *Some sort of whore.* Mom shook her head. "He's right, Lottie. That dress is a goddamn invitation. Go change." I'd had no idea, in that moment, what I might possibly be inviting.

I remember Dad catching a Whitesnake video on MTV, Tawny Kitaen dancing on the hood of some car. Andy had turned it on, was practically drooling, but Dad pointed at me and said, "That's nothing but cheap," as though I were the one doing the splits, turning my come-hither eyes toward the long-haired glam rockers.

Later, when celebrity gossip told us Tawny's marriage was on the rocks, Mom nodded like she'd known it all along. "She'll have a hard time finding anyone else with that reputation. Don't forget, Lottie. You are the choices you make." I think about that all the time, the impossible bar Mom set for me when I was nothing but a confused teenager, all my inevitable bad choices still ahead of me.

During the molasses flood, we got stopped behind a blockade of fire trucks, police cars, even an ambulance, though the lights weren't on and the paramedics were outside, standing around with everyone else, shivering. We joined half the town, all of us out of our cars, lined up along the edges of the flow, mesmerized, speechless. Molasses fumes and frigid air stung the inside of my nose. Dogs barked in the distance. I drug my toes, pinched into Andy's old moon boots, across the cold asphalt of the road. The molasses had picked up a worn tennis ball, the soft green fuzz almost glowing against the amber liquid. I felt an urge to grab that tennis ball, to rescue it, but I didn't want to go knee deep into the molasses. Mom shivered, and I did too, imagining myself trapped in the suckery flow, the entire town watching from the sidelines, all of us sick from the fumes, from the inevitable sticky mess.

Our town, Loveland, makes a big deal about Valentine's Day, like it somehow belongs to them, like if you name a place for love, there will be more love there, which is objectively ridiculous. It still happens, a tradition. The Rotary Club sells big red plywood hearts in town every February, and you can pay to have things like *Liz and Albert 20 years* or *I ♥ Tony* spray-painted on them in white stencils. Dad didn't get Mom a heart, that year or any year, and I hadn't told her that my boyfriend, Jason Alles, had paid the thirty dollars to get one for me.

"Don't expect anything else," he had said. "This is Valentine's and your birthday—two birds, one stone." The heart said *Jason + Lottie 4-eva*, and the 4-eva part wrapped anxiety like iron chains around my heart. Jason had been my first kiss, New Year's Eve, and now he wanted sex. He'd started out with sweet, declarations of love, *I'll take care of you, baby*, but the longer I held out, the meaner he got. *There's plenty of girls calling me, Lottie, who know a lot more than you.* I knew what Mom would say, that I'd invited this, that I'd put myself in this position, that I'd already made myself that kind of girl. Still, I wanted something from her, some pearl of wisdom I could use. I didn't want to give Jason up. Mom was lost in some sort of funk, and Andy was nearly as mean as Dad. Jason's attention came in like high tide just as my family receded. Mom never gave me the language I needed for that moment, and I was too young to learn to speak it on my own.

"Hey Mom," Andy said, pointing up at my heart, "check out what Lottie's loser boyfriend did."

Mom looked long enough to register, but then her eyes dropped back down toward the molasses. The road was a mess of molasses and debris from the trash piles outside the mill, old fence posts, broken pieces of brick, warped brake rotors, a box spring. All of it was soaked, coated, heavy and disgusting—sticky as all hell. I willed my mother to look my way, save me, show me how to save myself. She grabbed my arm hard then, pulled me back from the crowd in slow, smooth motions so that nobody would notice a thing. It was everything I wanted, her full attention.

"You're smart enough to know better than Jason Alles," she said. "That whole family is nothing but trouble." I'll never forget how cold Mom was in that moment, the ominous scratch of her whisper, the absolute threat it contained. "And I'll tell you what else. If you get pregnant, Lottie, I'm going to make you keep that baby. And it will Ruin. Your. Life."

Maybe Mom was terrible in that moment, but I was too. "You're just jealous," I said. "If you are your choices, then how do you explain Dad?"

You can't take words like that back, Mom's or mine. They are always something you said, forever.

Mom turned her back to me, rejoined the crowd. The molasses was slowing as it cooled, settling in. It captured the pattern of the sunlight and lightened in honeyed rays. It was as hard to look away as it was to keep looking. My breath left my body as a howl, but I must have been the only one who could hear it, because nobody but Mom took any notice of me.

Mom would never recognize herself in my story, but that doesn't make it less true. There are some floods that threaten to suck you under, carry you away, and some floods that trap you in a way of thinking. Mom has both her feet in molasses, stuck forever with the version she tells herself, which is that she did everything she could to protect me, that she was always carrying me up some tree, that I was always, always, resisting her.

IF YOU WANT TO hike in Rocky Mountain National Park in the summer, it's best to rise early, beat the crowds. The sun was just up when Mom and I parked outside the Wild Basin Ranger Station, cinched up our hiking boots. A mangy-looking coyote scampered across the trailhead and disappeared into the pines. An invisible mountain bluebird sang its dawn song, unmistakable in its repetition: one clear high note and then a trill down the scale. The plan was to make it to Calypso Cascades, not quite two miles, one-way. I only ever chose the out-and-back routes now, no more loops. With Mom, I needed shortcuts, a clear way back.

"Morning, Lottie. Beth." Ed Mayne was a park ranger, mom's age but hearty, rugged. Ed and I weren't always in the same trainings at work, but when we were, I liked to sit next to him. I liked the way he crossed his arms in front of his chest, glared at whichever bureaucrat was leading the trainings, started almost every contribution he made with "With due respect" in a tone that made it clear he had no respect at all. "Keep an eye out this morning. Got reports of an aggressive moose near Copeland Falls."

"Bull?" Mom asked.

"Cow," Ed said. "Twin calves."

Mom and I both nodded, waved Ed away. We started along the

trail, silent except for Mom's wheeze, which she gets now with any movement, walking from the living room to the carport, from the bedroom to the kitchen. She hides her pesky cough well enough so far by sucking on LifeSavers. There on the trail, I saw her double up, pineapple and cherry at the same time.

"You're going to rot your teeth," I said. "Isn't there another way?"

Mom laughed, a cackle. "My teeth," she said, shaking her head. "Only you, Lottie."

"I'm worried," I said, knowing it was the wrong thing to admit. Mom saw worry as a sign of weakness. Worry has no place in the tough love philosophy.

"I'm not going to live long enough for my teeth to matter."

"You could," I said, my own heart suddenly ponderous and full, my own systems blocked. There was a rustling in the brush. A cold patch of air, the kind that gets trapped by conifer needles, dislodged and passed over us both. Mom shivered. We both turned, expecting an angry moose, but whatever it was, it was invisible to us.

"Lots of ways to deal with this, Lottie," Mom said. "Denial's the worst choice." Her voice was harsh, her eyes rolled, and I felt my belly sinking away from my lungs. I have always hated the way she speaks to and about me at the same time, the way she has of making me feel small and ashamed even when I know better. I thought then, as I had so many times before, that if she were not my mother, I would not spend time with her at all.

We arrived at Copeland Falls, snowmelt water tumbling off low boulders into a churning pool of white water, the river flow gentling quickly as the bed widened, smoothed. It's a small waterfall, relative to others, the crash and foam still loud enough that we had to half shout to be heard above it. All but the loudest noises in the forest drop into the rush of the water, which focuses any scattered sensory attention on the unrelenting press of water against rock.

We weren't even a half mile from the trailhead. Mom had gone pale, her dry cough muscled past the candy. We sat on a downed tree, and she covered her mouth with a white bandanna. When she pulled it away, the phlegm was tinted pink.

"From the candy," she said. I wanted to shove her own words back into her mouth, ask her who was in denial now, but instead I pulled her into a side hug, felt her body relax into mine.

"Mom," I said, "I'm pregnant."

Her shudder ran electric along the side of my body. "By who?" Which was of course the first thing she would say.

"Ed Mayne." Not that I hadn't thought about it, with Ed. I'd made honest efforts with the other available men in the canyon. It was a shallow pool, sparsely populated. There were plenty of moments when Ed looked just as good as anyone else.

Mom pushed away from me then, her eyes flashing. "That old goat. He knew you in diapers."

"I'm kidding," I said, waving my hand uselessly in the air, giggling, feeling my face burn red. Mom's lips were pursed, no hint of smile in her whole body. "Jesus, Mom. It's not Ed. It was a cowboy passing through town with the rodeo last month. A one-night thing."

"A cowboy?"

"What? He was." I had no plans to tell her about his wedding ring. He hadn't bothered to take it off, and I had been so grateful for his rough hands on my belly, my thighs, for the respite from my wholly unintentional celibacy, that I didn't ask questions.

Silence. Mom was stone-faced. I felt desperate, fluttery. I wanted to be able to describe the thorny truths of my life, to have Mom accept them without judgment.

"You seem a little old for a lesson in contraception," Mom said.

"Shit happens, Mom."

"If you let it, Lottie."

I stood then and walked toward the water, arched my back into a stretch. I caught the staggered song of a dipper bird, its joyful bouncing along the river's edge. Dippers make hunting look like dancing, keep their life requirements playful. There's a lesson in it. I took a deep breath, turned back toward Mom. "You're not even a little happy?" I asked.

"That's not the point," she said. "This is a hard road you're on. You need to find this rodeo clown. For the money, if nothing else."

"Cowboy, Mom. Not clown."

"You think you can do this all alone?"

I thought of the pink phlegm on Mom's bandanna, the fluid collecting around her ankles, her congested, gummed-up heart. "Looks that way," I said. "Looks like I don't have much of a choice."

"Look harder," Mom said, doubling over into a coughing fit gone totally out of control, and I added this reaction to my list of things I want to forgive but can't.

I HAD SEX WITH Jason for the first time underneath a set of bleachers on the football field. The early crocus bulbs were in bloom, the grass starting to green its way out of dormancy, but the nights were still frosty, cold air that burned bare skin. I'd snuck out. I remember that it hurt but not that bad, that Jason made fun of me for not knowing how to manage a condom, that the bright white of the moon seemed ominously far away and too close, moonlight so bright it blocked out the stars. Back home, I hid under my bedcovers, thinking that was it, I'd never get to have that night again, my virginity gone forever to the wrong boy in the wrong way. I felt all the shame I'd been taught to feel, resigned to the loss, bound by it, like that one yes meant yes to every future encounter, like I'd lost the right, somehow, to say no ever again. *You are your choices.* I took a bath so hot my skin stayed red for an hour after.

Mom was at the kitchen table with a plate of buttered toast and a mug of black coffee, watching a squirrel devour the seeds she'd put in the bird feeder.

"Morning, Mom," I said. Everything felt awkward, new, like I had been taken apart and reassembled, all my joints just a little off where they once were.

"Sleep well?" Mom asked.

I scanned her face, trying to see what she knew, what she guessed, but she was inscrutable.

"Not really," I said.

Mom smiled, shrugged, turned back to the window. Nothing was going to happen. I didn't know whether the adrenaline rush I had then was terror or relief.

Jason took to coming over pretty much every night. My room was in the basement. I'd unlock the back door after Mom went to sleep. We'd have hushed, quiet sex, and he'd sneak back into his room before his dad got home from the night shift. I wanted it until I didn't want it anymore. It felt like something separate from me, like I was watching an unrecognizable movie version of myself. I have trouble explaining all this, even to myself, even now, until I remember that I was only fifteen. There's no explaining the naked human frailty of fifteen.

I tried saying no one time, but Jason put his hand over my mouth, entered me anyway. I know he heard me, but he never acknowledged it, and I didn't confront him. After that, it was less heartbreak to pretend I wanted it than to say no, have to endure him taking it anyway.

At school, Andy punched my shoulder. "Heard you been writing love letters," he said, "heard they're all about how much you love having Jason Alles inside you."

I had to struggle to stay upright, fight the urge to curl my whole body around the tightening I felt in my gut. "I didn't write that. I wouldn't ever." *Jason. Jason wrote it.* I knew the truth of it right away, what it meant for my reputation.

Andy was a natural skeptic, but I think he recognized something honest in my reaction. "You swear?"

"Of course I swear. Who do you think I am?"

"Not the same as I thought you were yesterday," Andy said. "Nobody thinks of you the same as they did yesterday."

I nodded, prepared myself to absorb this new person the world believed me to be. I didn't confront Jason, because it was exactly what everyone always told me would happen, something I believed I deserved. I watched the crocus fade, the daffodils and tulips bloom, the buds on the tree branches swell and pop open, the dandelions, half bright yellow beauty, half jagged green weed, carpet the backyard, where the neighbors couldn't see them. I started leaving the door locked so Jason would have to knock on my window, make a racket. I craved the day Mom would walk in on us, the day she would show me how to end it. I wanted a reboot of Mom's flood story, wanted her to drag me, screaming, ungrateful, into the safety of the pines.

And then I woke up one morning and Jason was still there, and it was a Saturday, and I heard Mom awake upstairs, shuffling around.

"Get out," I whispered. "Go home."

"Stop freaking out," he said, rushing into his clothes.

He climbed out the window and made a run for it. It was full light, and I imagined Mom at the kitchen window, watching Jason's sprint across the yard scatter the birds from her feeder. I dreaded going up there. Also, I couldn't wait.

It was worse than I had imagined, both Andy and Mom at the table. It was impossible to believe they hadn't seen him.

"Mom," I said. My voice caught on the tears in my throat.

There was a long pause. *Say something,* I thought, *let's do this.* I wanted the dam to break. I needed flooding, aftermath, a cleanup effort.

She wouldn't meet my eyes. She carried her plate and her mug past me into the kitchen. She ran water into the sink for a long time. She said, finally, "I'm not feeling well today," and she disappeared into her bedroom.

Andy looked me over—his face made me think he'd stolen all my anger, that if I had half his fire I could burn down the world. "Well shit, Lottie," he said.

I wish I could say that Mom's refusal to act taught me valuable lessons about how to handle my own business, that I managed to teach myself how to gracefully end a relationship, but it was Andy who took action, a story people started telling again when he went on trial. Jason was using the band saw. Andy struck up a casual conversation, and the next thing everyone knew, the tip of Jason's index finger was on the floor, the sawdust below it expanding, absorbing the blood that ran, then dripped, then balanced in a fat drop on the edge of the machine. Andy swore it was an accident, and that's where the consensus seemed to land. Mr. D, the teacher, put Jason's finger on ice and drove him to the ER, but they couldn't stitch it back on, so Jason was left with just half an index finger. It looked remarkably like a canned sausage. People started calling him "Little Smoky," and he stopped calling me.

Jason slipped out of my life after that, and now Andy has too, but that's not how it works with mothers. Mom and I have never spoken about that day, about any of those days. I'm stuck with my mother, which sticks me with the version of myself that I am when I'm with her, which swallows all the other, better versions.

I TOOK THE JOB in Denver, moved Mom to a hospice facility across the street from the hospital where I had my baby. Leah took

Tyler for at least one visit, a kindness for which I will always be grateful. Mom gave the nurses book recommendations, cheerful reprimands about their diet soda habits.

I had only just found my own feet, the air of the city fresh in my lungs, when I delivered my Willa, alone, the doctor an efficient man I had never met before. All the nurses said Willa was a good baby, and I thought, *Of course she is. She's the best baby.* She latched onto my breast on her first try, didn't cry unless she needed changing. Even now, she isn't fussy, my Willa. She slept for four hours straight the night I spent in the hospital, and even though the nurses told me to sleep when the baby slept, I couldn't. Birthing Willa was thrilling, made me feel invincible. It took days to come down off the adrenaline rush. That first night in the hospital, Willa swaddled in a cotton blanket, her sweet head covered in a soft knit hat, I got out my computer to send Andy a picture.

I was surprised to see an email waiting from him. *Heard from Mom. Thought up some names for the bastard children of sad rodeo clowns: Giggles. Wally. Tex. LOL. Just kidding, sis. Congratulations, I guess.*

I didn't send a picture. I couldn't put my Willa next to that ugliness, wanted to shield her forever from any kind of cruelty, especially anything that would make her connect her sense of herself to my reputation, to any reputation at all. People will believe whatever they want to believe, about themselves and others both. I think the key is teaching her to see it without making her feel responsible for it, but for that I need an entirely other version of myself.

They discharged us the next day, and I pushed Willa in her stroller across the street to meet Mom, too sick and weak now to leave her room. It hurt to walk. I was still in the mesh underwear, the supersized postpartum maxi-pad, but the sunlight was warm on my face, the world bathed in brightness. Even Mom had the blinds up, the sunshine glare through the windows obscuring the numbers on her monitors, illuminating the mysterious tubes that had been, for weeks now, working to make her death as comfortable as possible. I believe, even now, that Mom lived long enough to meet Willa out of the sheer strength of her will. Mom's love was never enough for me, not even at the end, but it was ever-present, which is something.

I elevated Mom's bed to get her into a sitting position. She had oxygen tubes in her nose and an IV in her left arm, but she still held Willa, snuggled her close, clucked and cooed like a mother hen.

"She's beautiful, Lottie," Mom said, her tears flashing like silver in the sun.

"Her name is Willa," I said. "Like Cather. These things happen when your grandmother is a librarian."

Mom smiled then, a sincere smile, real happiness. The light hit Willa's face and she sneezed a delicate, tiny sneeze. Mom pulled my girl close to her chest so that her face was out of the sun.

"Goodness," Mom said, smiling. "Bless you, little one." She was almost singing, her voice so soft, so loving.

There, in her hospice room, I wrapped Willa in the quilt Mom used to haul me up the tree, all those years ago, nursed her in the rocker as Mom napped in the sunlight warmth. There was no deathbed apology, no dramatic airing of grievances, the same way we never saw the mama moose that day on the trail. There was no confrontation to settle whether I would have used my body to shield her from danger, whether she would have done the same for me. Mom had her flood story, and I had mine, and when I realized that I didn't have to reconcile them I could feel the air move again, let them both go with something close to grace. When I think of Mom now, when the heavy ache of missing her is hard to carry, I choose my images carefully. I picture Mom asleep in her hospice bed, holding Willa like a treasure, the light that was, on that one day, everywhere around her.

Natural Resource Management

—

LEAH HAD BEEN PROMOTED out of any requirement to drive through the Riverside Open Space construction site every morning—her job now more planning than boots-on-the-ground crew supervision. But her boy, Tyler, three years old, loved coming to Riverside, and she loved sharing it with him—the transition from neglected industrial landscape to half-wild, half-cultivated multi-use public land. It had been Leah's idea, years before, to convert the old quarry to open space, her map of the trail system and the accessible fishing piers, her list of native aquatic plants grown specially for habitat, her deal with the Colorado Division of Wildlife to stock the ponds with perch, with bluegill, with bass, to build launch pads for float tubes. In a few days, Leah would sign off on project completion, and the open space would fill with fishermen, joggers, dog walkers, amateur painters, birders and naturalists checking species off their life lists. Until then, she could arrive before the work crews and present the urban wilderness to her son like it belonged to them, like they alone owned this beauty.

She could drink her coffee while the clouds morphed and shifted above her, while the moon faded and her own pride in this work glowed like the sunrise.

This morning, she could see that the unusually steady rains of the past few days had been transformational—the cottonwoods and peachleaf willows bogged down as they took on fall color, sagged toward the river that ran high for September, brown and churning like the June rise, still well within its banks despite the flash flood warnings coming over the radio. The world outside was oddly hushed, rain muting the usual honking of Canadian geese, the rustle of rabbits scurrying into the brush.

The wipers on her truck were high-speed manic over Tyler's soft murmuring from the crew cab booster seat. Leah was always relieved when he was in a happy mood. He'd been a difficult birth, a colicky baby, a toddler prone to run and hide in stores if she looked away for even one second, the kind of loud, at three, that made elderly women raise their eyebrows, purse their lips, the kind of loud that the teachers at his new day care frequently mentioned at evening pickup. Tyler jumped down from the truck and zigzagged from puddle to puddle, stomping his mud-booted feet, his broad smile all delighted sunshine. Everything Tyler felt—delight, frustration, joy, anger—he felt all the way and out loud.

"Mommy! Fish!" Tyler pointed and shrieked. Leah looked up to see an osprey struggling with a fresh kill, gaining altitude until it finally made the nest. It had been Leah's idea to place a plywood board in the high branches of a dead cottonwood to lure ospreys to Riverside. In late spring, she had caught the white breast of a male making graceful, laconic swoops with a river fish in his talons, descending toward a haphazard nest built of sticks and twigs on her platform, his teakettle chirping attracting Leah's gaze easily as it attracted the female who eventually chose him. Now, she and Tyler monitored the young in the nest.

Leah had a degree in natural resource management, spent her days considering ways to improve the collective quality of life — juggling the competing demands of resource extraction and recreation, considering fair allocation, providing access to nature so more people would come to love it as she did, work harder to protect it, take loud, passionate action to save the whole dying world. She'd grown up fishing these ponds as a girl, back when it was still an abandoned quarry. She'd learned to chase shots and kiss boys under the old cottonwoods in high school. She'd mummied herself into her sleeping bag and slept outside on the pond banks, dreaming of a future as bright, as dramatic, as the night sky constellations. She wanted to give her boy all the best she herself had gotten from this place, wanted him to know he had roots in this ground, wanted him to feel the way those roots could nourish and support him. In truth, Leah needed her own constant reminders of what these roots were worth. Roots were also binding, stuck deep, they kept her static through the aftermath of catastrophes past, an easy target for future catastrophes.

"I'm hungry, Mommy." Tyler had lost interest in the osprey, was pulling tufts of buffalo grass out in clumps.

"Want me to get you a fish?" she said, leaning her own smile close to his, flexing her fingers like talons.

Tyler copied her, but he grabbed both her cheeks with his talon fingers, squeezed too hard. He was always taking the game too far. Leah wondered how she should even begin to teach him to notice the boundaries people made for themselves, lines he was always crossing, without damaging his sense of himself in the world. She thought how small his heart must be. How fragile. "No fish. Treats!"

"Okay, buddy. Treats it is."

Tyler helped her with his car seat straps, went back to playing calmly with his Hot Wheels cars. She turned the key in the ignition, took one final glance around the site. It took time and patience to calibrate the balance of a disrupted system, to discern which investments would yield an optimal outcome. She had spent years working through the Riverside project, which everyone agreed was a success, but she had yet to figure out a way to apply these principles to the tattered remnants of her family life. It had been months since she'd been to a coffee shop, since she'd been anywhere but Tyler's day care, work, the small courtyard playground in their apartment complex. People looked at her differently now—suspicious, judgmental, sometimes pitying. Leaving her apartment for any reason, she considered disguise—*I could wear a mask. Pull a sheet over my head. Find a convincing false mustache*—but the anonymity she craved more than anything was impossible to expect. Everyone in this town knew her business. Everyone was some kind of witness. Still, she wanted the sweet vanilla syrup, the creamy thickness of whipped cream on her tongue. She wanted the tiny vases of carnations—pops of color against the gray, clouded light, the local art like rainbow magic on the wall. Like Tyler, she wanted a treat, a small pleasure, a baby step back toward normalcy.

THE COFFEE SHOP WAS just as she remembered it—cozy, half crowded, the layered smells of coffee and baked goods oily and deep. The baristas, a rotating cast of local teenagers with big-city aspirations and acid wit, were flirting for tips. Leah felt her heart rate slow, her breathing normalize. *See? Nothing to be afraid of.* Tyler pressed his face against the glass of the bakery display, his eyes glittery, overwhelmed at the choices in front of him.

"Blueberry muffin," he said, and his face registered such joy when he held the treat in his own two hands that Leah nearly laughed out loud. She ordered a latte and was feeling a sense of accomplishment until she saw Bobby Jackson and his dad, Elmer, staring at her from a corner table, and then the days and days of rain, rain near impossible for Colorado, rain like three monsoon seasons, seemed to dampen the whole café, everyone suddenly on edge. *I could grab Tyler and run. I could just go and never ever come back.* But Bobby was walking toward her, his face unreadable, and her body, gone stiff, did not respond to her brain's frantic flight signals.

"Haven't seen you around, Leah." She found it unsettling, Bobby's calm, like there was nothing difficult between them.

"Can't imagine you saw the front page this morning." Elmer joined them, handing her a copy of the local newspaper. "Can't imagine you'd be out in town today if you had."

"Dad," Bobby said, but he didn't make eye contact, not with Leah, not with Elmer.

"Can I have a donut?" Tyler's face was sticky, his shirt covered in crumbs.

Leah lifted him onto a nearby chair. "Eat your muffin, buddy." She looked at the newspaper and rubbed both her eyes. The feeling was familiar, half shame, half anger, an ache in her gut like a battered funny bone, a pain she couldn't keep herself from coming back to, over and over, even when she was alone. The article was an exposé of the case, a year ago, that had sent her now ex-husband, Andy, a police officer, to prison. Andy had become convinced that Bobby, an old friend of theirs from high school, a friend to everyone in town, was cooking meth in the abandoned sugar mill that Elmer had bought cheap at the auction after the bankruptcy. There had been months of surveillance before Andy finally called in the SWAT team, who'd found nothing but some old Mason jars full of suspicious powder and a room full of flea-bitten jackrabbit pelts.

"That's sugar," Elmer had said. "The whole place is full of sugar." But Andy said the rapid test he did on-site showed meth, put Bobby in handcuffs, left every window in the old mill office Bobby had been living in shattered, the doors torn off their hinges. Bobby spent a week in jail until the sample they'd sent down to the lab came back positive for insect wings and dust mites and, yes, sugar, but not a single trace of meth. Bobby was released but he'd been shaken, gone jumpy. A junior officer reported abnormalities on the scene, and Andy was found to have rigged the rapid test. The investigation found planted evidence, missing evidence, irregular evidence in other cases Andy had been on, and he'd been in prison now for six months. Elmer had rented a crane, bought a bunch of paint, and written a life-sized message across the roof of the old mill: *It was sugar, stupid!*

Bobby and Leah had been close since grade school, her parents friends with his. Even now, he hadn't blocked her on Facebook, which she considered some kind of miracle. Growing up, she'd had cake at Bobby's birthday parties, beaten him and Elmer both at horseshoes at her high school graduation party. When Leah first went to work for the city, Elmer hadn't seemed bothered by the fact that she was a lady with opinions and decision-making power, and the other men who might have resisted her followed his lead. Leah's own parents had moved to Florida—day-drinking on the beach, skin like leather purses—and Elmer and Marcia, his wife, had been something like backup parents. When Tyler was born, they'd come to visit with a card, a hand-knit baby cap.

In the aftermath of everything, Leah had filed for divorce, been awarded full custody, and promptly gone into hiding. She hadn't seen Bobby or Marcia, only Elmer, at work, where he had become far less cooperative, if not openly cold. There was no way to quantify how much they blamed her. Leah, in the absence of other information, assumed Andy had ruined everything, and Elmer and Marcia, and Bobby too, probably, would never, ever forgive her.

Tyler threw the empty muffin paper onto the floor of the coffee shop and started screaming. "I want a donut!" he shrieked. "A DONUT!"

He crawled under the table, still wailing a deep harmonic

undertone to the raindrops that tapped heavy, battered by wind, against the windows, the glass door. One of the baristas widened her eyes, shook her head slightly, and another covered a smirk. Elmer nudged Bobby with his elbow. Bobby turned his face away so that Leah couldn't tell what reaction he was hiding.

A headache was building behind Leah's right eye. *If I buy him the donut to shut him up*, she thought, *they'll say I've spoiled him*. Tyler turned up the volume. "I hate you," he said, snot and tears shining like glaze on his cheeks. "I want Daddy. I want a donut."

Leah tried to look competent—no, capable. She needed to look capable. Why did he have to behave like this? *He's only three*, she told herself, *he can't help it*. She put her coffee on the table, got down on all fours. Heat prickled up her spine, shame roared conch-noise in her ears. *Neither can I, I guess*.

"Need help?" Bobby asked. Elmer snorted, shook his head. The other customers were staring, the baristas rolling their eyes, whispering.

"Got it, thanks." What she wouldn't give now to rewind the morning, stick to the routine, be satisfied with her homemade coffee, with the ospreys, with the parts of the world she could still move comfortably through.

Tyler pushed himself farther away from her, still screaming. When she got close enough, he grabbed her arm and bit her. He didn't break the skin, but Leah gasped, pulled her arm away so forcefully that Tyler fell backward, hitting his head on the tile with a loud crack. Leah was horrified, overwhelmed with guilt, and then Tyler began to repeat the motion, repeatedly banging his head against the floor. *For God's sake*.

"Jesus," Elmer said.

Leah grabbed Tyler then, rougher than she was proud of. Cross-legged on the floor, she pulled him into her lap and tried to calm the anger and the fear and the rising helpless darkness these fits evoked in her heart, hoping that might, in turn, calm her boy. She took a breath for control, counted slowly to three, tried to listen to the soothing patter of rain on the dark windows.

When her voice could paint a veneer of calm over her anger, she said, "No biting, buddy. We don't bite people. It hurts."

Tyler was flailing, trying to land his little fists on her neck, her face. She pulled him close to her, trying to mask the half-panic in her voice as she said, over and over, "I'm here with you, buddy. I love you. You can calm down."

"He always like this?" This from Elmer. No mercy.

"Dad, he's just a little guy." Bobby looked concerned, tense, on the verge of reaching toward her.

"We just need a minute," Leah said. "He just needs to settle."

Tyler threw his head backward into hers, catching her jaw, and Leah worked to loosen her shoulders, untense her muscles, breathe through the pain. When Tyler was like this, she felt she had to constrain him, to wrap herself around him, mother as shield, or mother as straitjacket, but she couldn't put herself between his rage and his heart, and she couldn't blame him either. Even as she tried to settle her boy, she knew she was holding him here in her anger at least as much as she held him in her love. She kept her head turned away from the baristas, away from Elmer and Bobby. Refusing to acknowledge them felt a tick closer to privacy. Leah wondered at this all the time—the amount of comfort you could manufacture for yourself even when there was no tangible change in your situation.

Finally, Tyler calmed, settled into her lap. Spent, he turned, wrapped his arms around her neck, snuggled his snot-slick nose against her skin. His head was heavy on her shoulder as she lifted him. She left her coffee on the table, nauseated by all the bitterness. She nodded a goodbye to Bobby. She dropped the newspaper in Elmer's lap.

"I'm not Andy," she said. "You should know better."

Her heart rattled from adrenaline, from an impulse to throw her own body on the floor, let her flailing limbs pound the tiles, let her screams terrify the community. But instead, she'd drop the boy at day care and go to work. The tantrums she faced there, thrown by grown-ass men, were less frequent and much more easily managed.

SHE DROPPED HER UNSETTLED boy at day care, drove away trying to parse the emotions contained in the wild look that had flashed into his eyes and disappeared. It was still early when she returned to Riverside, but Elmer was already on-site, waiting to complain, probably. Thinking up ways to make her job harder. He was unavoidable. She rolled down her window, cocked her head, and waited for him to say something.

"You still planting those aquatic seedlings today?" Elmer asked. He was wearing knee-high mud boots and a yellow rain slicker. He looked like an elderly Paddington Bear. The back of his truck was full of loose shovels, rakes, pitchforks with splintered wooden handles. Recently, Elmer had demanded weekly updates of construction plans and progress at Riverside, and someone above Leah's pay grade had agreed he should get them. Elmer had been the ditch rider since before she had started in the city planner's office, possibly since before she was born. The ponds at Riverside were fed by the irrigation ditches Elmer managed, snowmelt water from west of the Continental Divide pumped, against gravity, to the thirsty populations on the Front Range. Elmer could raise or lower the water levels in the ponds by opening or closing gates in a series of concrete weirs spread out over the site, weirs Leah was not allowed, legally, to mess with on her own.

Her crew, up against the deadline, would plant despite the rain, but she didn't want Elmer to feel high and mighty about knowing things. She shrugged. "When the site foreman gets here, you can ask him."

Elmer felt it his duty, as a citizen and as the longtime ditch rider, to make his opinions known. At any given time, half the city council was pissed at Elmer and half loved him. Keeping track of who was on which side could have been a full-time job in itself. Then again, plenty of people were pissed at Leah these days—the women at Tyler's day care, clerks at the grocery store, a few people at work who had resented her success anyway, but the change in Elmer cut deep. Leah knew she hadn't done anything wrong, that it was all incredibly unfair, but, as her mother had always told her, such was life. You shouldn't expect fair.

"I wouldn't plant anything today if I were you," Elmer said.

"How about you go do your job," Leah said, "and leave me to do mine." Elmer's face flushed red, and Leah felt satisfied. She'd known it would set him off.

"Lake Estes is near full. Likely they're going to start sending water down the river and into the ditch systems, relieve the pressure on the dam," Elmer said. "You're going to want those gates open if the ditches start flooding."

"We already negotiated the schedule, Elmer. I need those gates shut. If the water gets too deep, we'll have trouble getting those seedlings to take. New roots like that, they'll wash right out."

"What's that you just said about whose job is whose? I been managing these ditches since you were in diapers. I saw the damage of the '76 flood. You ought to listen to me."

"It's not personal, Elmer. It's just a deadline."

"It's your mistake to make, I guess."

Leah was exhausted. It wasn't her fault, she didn't think, that Tyler was so sensitive, or that Andy had falsified evidence in so many cases against people in town. She pictured her husband in an orange jumpsuit, wondered why it felt like so many people thought she should be wearing one too. *It would be so much easier to do this alone*, she thought, *if it didn't feel like Andy was still around all the time.*

Leah looked toward the river, toward the gates, caught the young ospreys jockeying for position in the nest—the firstborn, the biggest, always muscling the others away. She hadn't seen as much of the parents over the past few weeks—she assumed the birds were preparing for migration, weaning their chicks away from protection and provision. She wondered what it would be like to fly away herself, how hard she'd have to work to carry Tyler with her.

"What do you tell your boy? About his dad?"

Leah looked at Elmer. Her shock morphed into suspicion, but Elmer's face had softened into something closer to kindness, the Elmer she remembered from the before times.

"Not much. That Daddy had to go away." Leah felt tears rising but forced them back down. Not in front of Elmer. Not now. "I figure I have some time before he needs to know everything." Why she was trusting Elmer with even this small bit of information was unclear. She had so many questions and nobody to ask.

"He reminds me some of Bobby, when he was that age. Sensitive. Couldn't hardly keep up with him." Elmer got in his truck, started the engine. The ospreys startled at the noise. Leah wondered for the rest of the day, as she watched her crew plant the seedlings, watched them trim the roof on the new bathrooms, whether this was some sort of peace offering from Elmer, whether she'd just misunderstood him all this time, or whether he was changing the way he saw things. Maybe just saying it out loud, *I'm not Andy*, which had felt so tremendously good, had made a difference. She watched the river churn, ominous, watched it swell with torrents of rain, and then it was time to pick Tyler up from day care. Leah felt breathless, untethered, her life suddenly too much for one adult and a preschooler to manage.

WATER FROM THE ROOF gutter downspout rolled toward the storm drains outside the day care, the deluge spreading across the asphalt of the parking lot in large fan shapes, disappearing into the rushing temporary stream along the curb. Leah stomped her muddy boots on the mat, rang the bell, and waved into the camera at the secured entrance. It had always felt strange, this idea that Tyler was locked away from her, that she needed someone else's approval to get inside, close to her son. The receptionist said, "I guess we need the moisture," and though Leah didn't correct her, she knew that wasn't exactly true. The ground had reached saturation days ago.

Ms. Evers, the center director, stuck her head out of her office door. "Mrs. Tinker? Can we talk for a moment?"

Leah nodded. Was she being called to the principal's office? She felt an odd wave of shame, though she knew that was nonsense.

"Tyler doesn't nap," Ms. Evers said.

Leah laughed. "Tell me about it. Doesn't sleep much at night, either."

Ms. Evers raised an eyebrow. She did not return Leah's smile. "It's a rule here."

"How can you make a rule about napping?"

"State regulations state that the children must lie on a mat quietly for at least twenty minutes daily," Ms. Evers said.

"Sure, but that's different from napping. He hasn't napped since he was ten months old."

"All the other threes sleep, some of them for more than two hours. The room has to be quiet during nap time."

Leah caught the motion of the raindrops on the window, the way they landed in a tremble, suspended, stuck, before beginning their slow, meandering descent toward the sill.

"Isn't there somewhere else he could go while the other kids nap? An awake room?" Leah's mind conjured a picture of a panic room, thought maybe in this case the analogy held.

"Impossible."

"Seems less impossible than making a three-year-old stay quiet for two hours." Some things, Leah knew, simply could not be managed. Husbands who made criminal professional decisions. Children who were not tired in the afternoon. "I can't make him nap any more than you can."

"If the situation doesn't improve, we may have to pursue disciplinary action. Perhaps a suspension."

"You suspend preschoolers?" Leah struggled to square her vision of preschool—loving teachers singing repetitive songs, gently reminding the children that Play-Doh was not for eating, directing cleanup and story time—with the lack of compassion she felt these women had for her son. Would it be different if he napped? Were the tired children better loved?

"We reserve the right. It's policy."

Leah lifted Tyler into the air when she got to him, felt his belly against her chest, his little legs hugging her sides. She held him longer than normal. If she loved Tyler more, loved him better, maybe she could counteract the way the world saw him—the way she worried the world would make him see himself.

"Mommy," he said, his breath hot and vaguely sour on her neck, "it still waining?"

"Still raining, buddy. Let's go home."

HER NEW APARTMENT COMPLEX was fancy, had a community clubhouse with a pool and a weight room, but the walls were flimsy, porous, leaking not just the sound of the Broncos game on her neighbors' TVs but the dank smells of root vegetable soups from their kitchens, the artificial shampoo fragrances from their showers. Leah measured two cups of flour into a bowl, two tea-spoons baking powder, a shake of salt. She took a moment to feel the freedom of making pancakes for dinner without Andy's insistence that breakfast foods be served only before 10 a.m. "Like McDon-ald's," he had said, back before McDonald's started serving break-fast all day. "They know what's up. Shut that shit down at ten." Andy had a lot of strict rules like that. Andy would have sided with Ms. Evers. He believed that children only defied authority if you let them, had always been clear that any fault in their son was planted there by Leah's misguided loving permissiveness. Some of it, she thought, must have been Andy's fault. Andy worked the late shift, had been with Tyler all day while Leah worked. Questions of credit and blame had been heavy in their young marriage. It was a para-dox of single motherhood—the freedom to make all the decisions, and the heaviness of the worry that she might make the wrong ones.

Tyler was belly to linoleum, rolling a replica Lightning McQueen car in long arcs around his body, making quiet engine noises with his lips. Leah stepped out the sliding door, stood at the very edge of the covered deck, felt the mist of fog condense on her forearms. A brief respite from the rain, the promise of more in the dark clouds to the west. The chill damp of the air made her grateful for the warmth as she stepped inside.

"Come on, buddy," she said. "Dinnertime."

"No thank you," Tyler said.

Leah braced herself. "Wash your hands, dude. It's dinner. Not a choice."

Tyler scrambled up and ran into the living room, crouching behind the couch. "No," he said. "No dinner. Cars."

"You can play after dinner," she said. "Put the toy down and come eat now."

Tyler screamed, "Nooooo!" and Leah put her hands in her hair, squeezed her temples with her palms. Outside, angry chattering finches scolded the aggressive squirrel that had displaced them from the common-area bird feeder.

"Okay, son," Leah said. "You come out where I can see you, and you can keep playing."

Andy would have grabbed the boy, forced him into a chair, made his voice deep and loud to terrify Tyler into obedience. He would have kept his voice in a deep growl and said, to her, "You're gonna have to start laying down the law, Lee. If he walks all over you now, you're going to have some real problems when he's a teenager."

Leah couldn't handle another tantrum, did not want to man-handle her tiny boy again. She pictured Tyler ten years from now, newly teenaged, all his little boy emotions spreading awkwardly into a body sprouting hair, growing muscles. She pictured a body the size of Andy's looming, fragile, falling all to pieces. It was terrifying. She wanted to absolve herself of her son's intense behaviors, give in to the embarrassment, say to everyone, "He gets this from his father." More than absolution, though, Leah wanted to scrub Andy out of Tyler completely, wanted the half of him that was hers to swallow the half that wasn't. Andy erased.

Tyler sat in Leah's lap and ate a pancake while she read *Goodnight Moon*. As she tucked him into bed, he placed both hands on her cheeks, looked intently into her eyes, and smiled. Leah wondered about the tangled, ragged pulsings of difficulty that seemed, somehow, to amplify love, the way that love, amplified, confused rational planning.

"You think you can try to take a nap at school tomorrow, son?" She rested her forehead against his.

"No," he said, rubbing his nose against hers. "No nap."

"Okay, buddy." Leah wanted this moment to last, wanted to soak herself to dripping with her son's sweetness, store it up as a buffer against everything that was hard.

The nightly news showed pictures of Lake Estes swelling against the dam, the Adams Tunnel under Rocky Mountain National Park at capacity, the system able to work against nature for only so long. "If the rain keeps up the way it's supposed to," the weatherman said, "I don't see that we get through tomorrow without some serious flooding in the Big Thompson Canyon." Leah felt fear cap her heart like clouds obscuring the peaks on the Rockies. Elmer had tried to warn her. Riverside was right in the path of that flood, her vulnerable aquatic seedlings, her fledgling ospreys in their nest of twigs.

THE NEXT MORNING, LEAH dropped Tyler at day care early and went straight to Riverside. She would try to adjust the headgate, check the levels and flow measurements in the Parshall flume, manage the surge of water. *Screw Elmer Jackson, anyway, for being right.* The police were already blocking access to the Big Thompson river bottom, monitoring the water. The rain raced in rivulets on top of the saturated soil.

The blockade officer let Leah through to the site. "Watch yourself. They opened the gates up in Estes Park an hour ago." Leah felt panic rising, felt her shoulders lift, her belly tense. The river was cresting its banks, a churning, relentless press.

She couldn't get eyes on the osprey as she drove in, but there in the parking lot was Elmer Jackson's truck. She looked again at the river and deflated, hopeless. She took a minute to orient herself, squinting into the sheets of rain. She wanted to get eyes on Elmer, ask him what he thought he was doing out here all by himself, ask him why he thought it would make any difference at all. Was there any amount of effort, attention, love, that could protect a project, a human, a life from something like this?

She heard a shout then, turned to the south, caught what looked like a pitchfork spinning end over end before it dropped back behind the wall of pigweed and miner's candle that stood between her and the line of irrigation ditches. She clambered through the mud and weeds to see Elmer twisted awkwardly on top of the trash rack on the culvert that ran under the muddy road, his legs caught in different openings, his feet dangling just over the churn of high water.

"Jesus, Elmer," she said, rushing toward him, "you all right?"

"Hell no, I'm not all right," he said, gasping with effort and pain. He shook his head slowly. "Stupid."

Leah couldn't tell whether Elmer thought she was stupid for asking or if he was stupid for falling in.

The ground at the top of the culvert was sloped and uneven. On both sides of the grate were tall piles of decomposing moss that had invaded the ditch since the nitrogen bloom of July. Today's moss slumped on top of the pile, an almost neon green slime.

"Careful now," Elmer said. "The plants are wet and there's the mud. It's awful slippery, which is how I ended up here."

Leah crouched, grabbing at the top of the grate. She felt stable, well rooted in the situation. "You in good enough shape to climb out of there if I get you my hand?" she asked. "I don't know about all this mud." *And the water*, she thought, *the water is rising fast.*

"Think so." Elmer winced and blew his breath out, hard, as he stretched his hand toward hers. She planted her feet and prayed the mud wouldn't give way beneath her. She held his hand in both of hers and slowly, carefully planting each foot, started pushing herself backward, up the hill.

"Hold up hold up," Elmer said, and she froze, taut, while he wrestled first his right leg, then his left, out of the grate. "Think this left leg of mine is broken. Or close to it."

"Tell me when you're ready," Leah said, and when Elmer gave

the signal, she kept pulling. Once Elmer was clear of the culvert, there was the mud to deal with. She propped Elmer up, her arm across his back, her hand in his armpit. Halfway to the trucks, they sat down on a downed cottonwood. The rain slicked Elmer's yellow rubber coveralls. She had expected panic from him, or at least some outward show of pain, but he kept his face stoic. Once in a while, he'd step wrong, wince, cry out just a little, but she pretended not to notice. She knew what it meant to crave dignity in the face of mortification. She could give Elmer that now.

"You trying to die today?" Leah asked. "Why'd you come out here?"

"Like I said, you want these gates open, want that water to flow out of here as fast as possible."

The site was socked in with clouds, landmarks blurred by the steady rain. Leah tried to remember how it looked in the sunlight, the blue of the sky, the laconic drift of cumulus clouds. She heard a noise from her platform, looked up to see the osprey chicks, water-logged and miserable, shifting position in the nest.

"How bad is it going to be?" she asked.

"I think pretty bad," Elmer said.

Leah was glad of the cold rain on her face, which masked, she hoped, her tears at the thought of Riverside destroyed—her years of vision and management and work, everything she had imagined it could become—all of it washed out, washed away.

She stood up. "You get all the gates open?"

"Not the one I fell into."

"I guess I have to get you out of here," she said, but she didn't want to leave. She wanted to turn herself into solid brick and mor-tar, grow up to the osprey platform, root herself firmly into the wet clay, send the inundation around and away from her open space. She wanted to fight, but the rain came in sheets, the dam was already open, the system entirely indifferent to her puny desires.

She looked at Elmer, small but dry inside his yellow slickers. The ospreys had hunkered down, gone invisible.

"How long do we have?" she asked.

"Flood's still up top of the canyon," Elmer said. "We got at least an hour, maybe more."

"You think opening that gate will help?"

Elmer paused, shrugged. "Might be nothing can help."

"Wait here."

"Don't have much of a choice," Elmer said. "This leg."

Leah used the footprints she'd left to get back, trying to step as carefully as possible into the existing holes in the suckery mud. When she reached the weir, she paused, stuck her hand in the chilly ditchwater, tensed with the effort of keeping it still and steady while strong current swirled and pressed around it, tried to move it, carry it downstream. The water had risen, was already flowing up and over the concrete box. Leah found the wheel, leaned her whole weight into it, but could not force it open. She kept shoving against it, but her feet slipped out from under her. She fell twice so hard her shoulder made divots in the soggy mud. Toward the trucks, toward safety, she saw Elmer hunched and shivering where she'd left him, and then she felt everything at once. Guilt for making an injured Elmer wait. Fear that she'd lose control, topple into the water, disappear into it. Frustrated rage that she was not, in the end, strong enough to open the gate, to save the site.

"You get it open?" Elmer asked when she reached him, mud-covered and bedraggled.

"Stuck." Leah put her hands over her face in an effort to preserve her own dignity, but it backfired. She'd rubbed mud all over her own stupid self.

They limped, slowly, toward the trucks. Elmer said, almost tenderly, "You did all you could." He lifted himself, gingerly, into her passenger seat. The truck radio announced that the schools were closing. Buses that had dropped children off just a couple of hours ago had been sent to deliver them back home. The blockade officers agreed to park Elmer's truck on higher ground.

Elmer called Bobby, told him to meet them at the hospital. "Who's got your boy?" he asked, poking a finger at his phone screen.

"Day care," she said. "Guess I have to go pick him up."

Bobby met them at the hospital, and he and Leah helped Elmer into a wheelchair. Leah was anxious to get to Tyler now, to have her boy within range of her care and protection. Bobby put a hand on her shoulder. "I don't know what would have happened if you weren't there." Leah felt for a minute Bobby wanted something more from the moment, something that might have been, but couldn't possibly have been, a hug.

Elmer looked at her too. "You did good today, Leah. You did your best."

Leah felt her eyes welling and turned toward her truck, toward Tyler. She felt her blood churning the same as the river. It was humiliating, wanting so much to be forgiven, when the only thing she'd possibly done wrong was marrying Andy to begin with. Really, how could she have known he'd turn out so rotten? They'd had some happy years. Andy wrapping a blanket over her shoulders when she was up late studying, learning the exact amount of cream she liked in her coffee. Andy's deep connection, as deep as hers, to their hometown, a sense of shared responsibility, between them, to improve and defend it. In the end, none of those things had mattered as much as his inability to ever admit he was wrong, his misplaced fervent confidence that he knew more about the people around him than they knew about themselves. Even the worst people were sometimes tender. Even liars, or maybe especially liars, knew how to be kind. She felt an urgency so deep it stung, blood-borne, racing through her whole body, to get to her son. It was up to her to keep Tyler safe, today and forever. It was up to her to be sure he only ever manifested the best of his father, if he had to manifest Andy at all.

LEAH PRESSED THE BUTTON for the secured entry at the day care, and the receptionist said "Okay," but the doors didn't unlock. The gutters were overflowing, sending a stream of cold rainwater down her back, which pooled at her bra and released slowly, tiny drops zigzagging down onto the small of her back, wetting the waistband of her pants.

Leah stared at the security camera that she knew ran a feed right to the reception desk. They shouldn't be making her stand out here in all this rain, even though she was soaked through already, slicked with mud, a real sight, she was sure. She sucked in her breath, held it, and when she could not hold it anymore, reached for the button again. Before she pressed it, the woman's voice sounded on the PA. "I see you. Hold your horses."

Inside, she smiled, aware that she was leaving a muddy puddle on the floor. "I'm here for Tyler."

"You can head on back." The woman, clearly alarmed by Leah's near-drowned appearance, picked up her phone receiver.

Leah could hardly stand the smell of the day care—sour milk, sour diapers, Lysol sprays and hand sanitizers—and today it was so cold and clammy, tantrums in the background, baby screams. The kids were as unsettled as anyone else. She could not imagine how Tyler stood it at all, and then she remembered that he didn't, not really.

When she reached the classroom, she saw Tyler alone in one corner of the room, building a large tower of blocks. Two of the other three-year-olds were coloring with their teacher, and Ms. Evers, the director, was reading to four others. When Tyler's block tower crashed to the floor, she saw Ms. Evers flash a look of annoyance. "Tyler!" she said. "Be quiet!"

Tyler was looking at the pile of blocks that had fallen. He looked so heartbroken, and Leah had to fight the urge to run in and scoop him up right away.

"Tyler," Ms. Evers said, sternly, "did you hear me?"

The other kids at her feet looked at Tyler as though he were a mosquito, something annoying they could swat away without thinking.

And then Leah could not stand it anymore, could not bear to see her boy so lonely, so isolated, to see the adults in charge of his care modeling such uncaring behavior. She did enter the room then, sat down next to her boy, her body between him and Ms. Evers's group.

"Can I help you fix your tower?" she asked.

Tyler crawled into her lap, wrapped his tiny boy fingers in her ponytail. "You wet, Mommy."

"Mrs. Tinker," Ms. Evers said.

"I came to take him home because of the flood," Leah said, "but I'm unenrolling him, as of now."

"According to the contract, in order to unenroll him—"

Leah cut her off. "I know. Ten thousand papers to sign and some number of days you're going to charge me for anyway. I'm not doing that today. I need to get my boy out of here."

She lifted Tyler up. It was hard to walk away with dignity, soaking wet, carrying a three-year-old and a diaper bag, but Leah tried to at least keep her chin high, to meet Ms. Evers's eyes with defiance on the way out the door. "You're not very good at your job," she said, "if you can only manage it when it's easy."

Tyler, peaceful in his car seat, fell asleep on the way home.

Leah marveled at the height and rush of the river. The swirl of the giant puddles outside overwhelmed storm drains, the water halfway up the tires of the truck. The two of them spent the day of the flood together, Tyler snuggled against Leah's side, sucking his thumb. They lit the gas fireplace in the apartment, ate warm soup, read books by candlelight when the electricity went out. They stayed up late listening to the emergency warnings on her battery-powered radio, to the winds that rattled the window glass against its cheap frames.

WHEN THE SKY CLEARED, the Big Thompson flood was still there. Leah and Tyler walked with their neighbors to the barricades the police had erected on a high point above the riverbed. Riverside was somewhere under a deep layer of churning brown water full of debris—hissing propane tanks, twisted trampolines, downed ponderosas with their gnarled exposed roots. Leah could not believe that the town could be so immensely deep. It held so much more than she'd thought it capable of, and everything familiar underneath that churning water was certainly unrecognizable now.

Later, she navigated the barricades, found an open route to the hospital. Elmer's left leg was in traction, the top of the hospital bed propped up, the newspaper spread out in front of him. The air around him shimmered with restlessness.

"How you feeling?"

Elmer looked at the bag of donuts she carried, the boy she balanced on one hip. Leah wondered whether this was going to work, this peace offering. She wouldn't be making it except for a vague sense she had that they'd found their way back to each other, that she could forgive him for blaming her, that he'd forgiven her as well.

Some time passed before he spoke. "You're pretty lucky Marcia's gone home. I'm not sure she'd abide a younger woman bringing me donuts in my vulnerable state."

"Oh," Leah said. How embarrassing. "I didn't mean . . ." but then she saw the twinkle in his eyes and relaxed, just a little.

Elmer grunted. She put the donuts on the nightstand next to the bed and sat down on the edge of a visitor's chair. Tyler sat on the cold tile, ran a Hot Wheels car along the metal bars under the bed. "Anything I can do to help?"

"Well, yeah," Elmer said. "I don't suppose you could close up all those Riverside gates when the water drops. I'm going to have some trouble getting out there for a month or so, at least."

"I couldn't even budge the one I tried yesterday."

"It's not rocket science," Elmer said. "Take some grease."

Elmer pointed to his jeans, which had been folded and laid neatly over the back of a chair. Leah tried to picture Elmer's wife, Marcia, worried, tired, folding the jeans, working from the assumption that daily care and maintenance of other humans, especially those who can't all the way care for themselves, is an intimate and powerful form of love.

"Keys in the pocket. I got a couple of the gates on padlocks."

She wanted to ask Elmer how he managed the heart-searing confusion of parenting, ask him for advice about how he would handle Tyler, his thoughts about sparing the rod, about how to talk to people who could not love her boy the way they were supposed to, about how she could be sure she loved him enough, that she loved him the right way. What should she do when people saw things in her boy that weren't there? How could she make rational decisions about something tangled so tightly around her heart?

Elmer handed Tyler a donut, met her eyes, didn't say a word. She didn't know what to make of what passed between them in that silence, but she felt understood.

DAYS LATER, WHEN THE water had receded fully, Leah put
Tyler in his car seat and drove to Riverside, the wreckage of five
years of her working life. She hadn't found a new child care center, didn't trust anyone with her boy, not anymore. She had been
taking him to work with her, assuring her boss it was just temporary, but she had no plan, not yet. The new parking lot at Riverside had been torn to pieces, the asphalt chunks found miles
downstream. The new roof on the bathrooms had been torn off.
Two large dumpsters were submerged in one of the quarry ponds.
The native aquatic plants had in fact been too young to withstand
the force of the water, and their tender roots had released and
washed away.

Bobby was there, skipping rocks into the pond, and Tyler, fas-
cinated, ran to stand next to him, to get a better view. Leah took a
deep breath. "Bobby, I don't know what—"

Bobby waved a hand to stop her. "It wasn't your fault, Leah.
I'm sorry for how it's been between us. I didn't know what to feel
about anything for a long time."

Leah sniffed. "Me either, I guess."

"Dad sent me down here to help you. With the ditches." He
still didn't look at her. Leah wondered if it was only her or everybody that Bobby couldn't face head-on. She didn't know how things
stood between him and Amy, his wife. She'd never thought about
how the town might have turned on him as well, never wondered
how he was feeling about his roots these days.

The three of them walked the site, trying to keep their feet on
the weeds and cheat grass, keep their boots from suckering down
into the sticky mud. One by one, Leah turned the wheels to close
the ditch gates. Only the one she could not move before the flood
needed any grease at all. The change in the levels, like so many
other things, was not immediately evident.

Tyler was throwing pebbles into the ditch, his laughter bright and loud. Bobby joined in, laughing too, the two of them suddenly oblivious to her presence.

Leah did not know the rules of raising a good man. She had doubts about how much influence any mother had on the heart of her son, but seeing Elmer and Bobby made her wonder how much influence any father had, either. She wondered how much of Andy she would see in her boy as he grew, whether Tyler would have the charm and youthful sweetness that had drawn her to Andy in the first place, what else would turn out to be innate to the boy, rigid, unmalleable.

The osprey nest had been above the high-water mark. The twig configuration of the nest was disheveled but intact. "Look, Tyler," Leah said, "do you see the nest?" She pointed at the tree. Tyler, enthralled with Bobby, with the deep splashing thunk of the rocks in the ditch, ignored her.

Bobby smiled, shrugged. "Kids, I guess."

There was no sign of the birds, not the parents or the juveniles. There was no way to know whether they had migrated into the storm, flown themselves free and clear, or been caught in the rushing misery, waterlogged, pulled into the churn and flow and press of the water. She didn't want to have to witness it alone. She didn't want to be the only one who wondered.

Leah lifted her boy, turned both their bodies toward the tree, and pointed again.

"There it is, son," she insisted. "Look. It's still there." Tyler turned away, refused to look in the direction she pointed. Leah gave in, wrapped both arms around Tyler, drew him close into herself, felt the tickle of his still-fine baby hair against her cheek. She began listing, silently, everything she could see was still standing, so much easier to bear than a list of everything that had washed away.

Lost Gun, $1,000 Reward,
No Questions

—

To: Mom
From: Charley
Subject: Project Gold Rush
August 18, 2016

Dear Mom,

Yesterday, Chris and I received a contract to install our hybrid hydraulic braking system in a national long-haul trucking fleet based here in LA. Also, we received a note from our former long-haul trucker of a father that read:

Boys—I'm out on a mining claim near Tonopah. Dying. You want to see me? Be quick. If I were you I wouldn't. But I'm not you. —Del

I said, right away: *Not our circus, not our monkeys, brother.*

Chris shook his head. He said we should first consider carefully, as always, the price versus the cost of the situation.

My brain was considering Del, but my heart was still at
your Colorado picnic table under the catalpa last October, the
checkered cloth under your mismatched dishes, black coffee,
ham steaks, the visceral mustard of Mary Lou Vargas's famous
potato salad. You were having one of your spells—do you
remember? When you're there but not there, riding the thermals of your own mind, spelunking through your darkening
memories? Either that or you were mentally rehashing what I
thought was an especially boring sermon that day. I gave you
my arm when you struggled up and down the church steps, but
I could have been Aunt Mano, could have been Chris, could
have been a wooden crutch. I felt wooden, for sure, puppet-
like, hard and cold and splintered. When I stood up, you stood
up too. The wind blew dried leaves off the tree, opening path-
ways to the sun so that it flashed like shagbark paparazzi, the
image of you impressed with light like a reverse X-ray, into and
through me, seared onto my bones.

You really looked at me then, and your eyes somehow twin-
kled pure blue, color flooding over the milky altostratus film
that has settled into them over the past years. Your eyes, for that
brief moment, were again blue like Chris's eyes, like your sisters'
eyes. The NOAA says that altostratus clouds are thin enough to
reveal the sun as if seen through ground glass. The NOAA says
altostratus clouds do not produce a halo effect, nor are the shadows of objects on the ground visible when they are present. The
NOAA dabbles in poetry, magic, and forecasting.

You smiled, placed your hands like cool velvet on both of my
cheeks.

I don't know who you are exactly, you said, *but I know I love you.*

Your old dog, Cass, started barking at an invisible squirrel.

Turn green, dog, you scolded. It's my favorite of your insults.

Do you see shadows on the ground, Mom? Or do you see only hazy sunlight as if through ground glass? What do these questions, these stories (if you can read them, if Mano reads them to you), make you feel?

Thomas Edison had a low opinion of Ouija boards. Chris has for some time been in possession of an original Frank's Box built by Frank Sumption, who loved dogs and chasing ghosts, and who himself passed on in 2014. Sumption modeled his boxes after the occult listening machines Thomas Edison built to try to prove the quackery of Ouija enthusiasts. Chris and I spent the past year building various iterations of Shack Hack devices, anticipating your death, but none picked up much otherworldly chatter on the AM dial. In truth, not even the original Frank's Box works. There are online communities devoted to Thomas Edison's views of the occult in the context of a wider spiritualist movement, his desire to scientifically quantify communication with the dead, and most of them would likely agree that the Shack Hacks that me and Chris built were real crappers, despite our collective advanced engineering degrees.

I have long admired Thomas Edison. I wonder what he would think, like I wonder what you think, about the recent societal discussions of neurotypicality across the human spectrum.

I love my aunts like mothers, Mano and Sister Agnes Mary. We are all of us kids a team effort, the product of the collective maternal efforts of you three sisters. But love like a mother is a pale simile for the way I love you, Ruth, my actual mother, for the way my heart went sonorous and resonant when you touched my face, deep music vibrating all through me, like a double bass.

When Chris pitches our hybrid hydraulic braking system to city managers and CEOs, he calibrates his emphasis on potential savings in price versus the potential savings in cost after he reads the room. For him, the faces reflect the degree of volatility in the oil markets, which is based on forecasts of an invisible future supply and demand, the degree of instability in the Middle East, or the possibly unsettling results of a long-shot presidential campaign. Beyond the sociopolitical factors, Chris, like all skilled salesmen, makes spot judgments about values and truth and bait.

It occurs to me that Chris sees me as a pale simile father, despite my lifetime of striving to be the man of the house (house being a metaphor now for family generally, for you and Chris, especially). I am only eight years older than him, after all, but how often did I hear that "man of the house" bit from you, from Mano, from Sister? I wish you'd understood then the way I imagine you do now, Mom, the ways that operated on me. I forgave you all eternally long ago in light of the many other ways you shaped me, but I wonder if this is one of your enduring memories: my little boy heart, earnestly beating, the three of you taking turns stacking responsibilities like lead weights upon it.

Maybe there's another sort of parent love out there, Mom, that Chris needs, and maybe Del is ready to give it to him.

Love, Charley

To: Mom
From: Charley
Subject: Project Gold Rush
August 19, 2016

Dear Mom,

The hydraulic braking systems we design and build capture
the energy of deceleration so that it can be applied to acceler-
ation, and when the price of gas is high, Chris describes elo-
quently the available cash savings in fuel alone. These days
of cheap gas, however, make price less of an incentive for
investment, so he emphasizes the costs. Lower fuel efficiency
could mean that Los Angeles, San Francisco, even Reno may
someday rival Delhi and Beijing for unlivable air quality, for
nature-deprived children with asthma and poor muscle tone.
Chris makes visible the connection between commercial vehicle
fleets and the melting ice caps, makes the suits believe he can
help them rescue a polar bear from drowning in an endlessly
warming Arctic waterway. He makes the polar bears personal.

This deep analysis of price and cost is one of many reasons
we should all be proud of Chris.

Thomas Edison was too difficult for public school. He was
home-schooled by his mother and father; the latter had been
thrown out of Canada for his firebrand, impolite politics.
Thomas Edison's father taught him critical thinking and distrust of government. Chris and I agree that our own father
taught us only distance: miles versus kilometers, synapse versus flesh, blood versus gasoline. Nevertheless, Chris wanted to
make an effort, so we did.

You might be surprised that I found Del's mine, surprised at
how I found it, but it's no surprise to me. We beat the LA traffic to the lonely Nevada highways today. The wind was steady

and relentless, shaking the low-lying sagebrush on the steppe, but not angry enough to disturb the sandy ground. Spirits and heat vapors shimmered above asphalt and desert alike. Cirrus clouds formed mare's tails in the shape of maiden's braids. Raptors rode the thermals far above—so far away I couldn't tell if they were eagles or vultures. Let's dispense with the portent of the obvious vulture symbolism. Let's say they were eagles for the sheer joy of siding with optimism, said optimism likely the difference between the success or failure of any quest—mythic or modern. Chris and Chris's phone stayed in the car. They were both impatient with me. I licked the tip of my finger and it came up from the earth crusted in sand, sparkling with flecks of mica. It tasted vaguely of strawberries—mostly like sucking on a penny. A grain of sand settled between my canine and my first premolar and remains impossible to dislodge. I have annotated your AAA map, perhaps beyond recognition.

Thomas Edison had an especially insomniac brand of genius. He took frequent short naps on lab tables, in his desk chair. Anywhere Thomas Edison felt sleepy, he went ahead and napped. Like Thomas Edison, like you, I am plagued by insomnia, but I am more successful at navigating through cloud triangulation than I am at napping. I feel like you might know what I mean by this, that you, more than anyone, understand me. Perhaps not. I wonder if you are still able to nap on humid summer afternoons.

The shadows stretched toward us first, then the signs themselves appeared near ground level on the side of the road. One was a Trump/Pence campaign sign. The other was handwritten on plastic board edged with federal safety yellow reflective tape, stuck with wires into the ground, waving gently (there was a breeze and a rather notable absence of the divine): *Lost Gun, $1,000 Reward, No Questions.* I pulled off the road, called the phone number listed, got the "voice mailbox is full" record-ing. A dirt road—rutted in some areas, washboarded in oth-ers, led back toward a looming range of desert mountains. A rusted old cattle panel blocked access, the *No Trespassing* sign was sun-faded, near illegible, but the chain and padlock that secured the fence to the post was shiny-new.

Chris said *no shit* and we both just knew this was the place Del wrote us about, and I tell you again, Mom, though I know you already know it, that sometimes just believing something is true—like that you'll find the father who left you—makes the thing solidify in the world, appear in front of you.

Jesus, Chris said. *How many found guns you think they have?*

It was late. We have returned to the effervescent antiseptic chlorine float of the Tonopah casino/hotel hot tub. Tomorrow we will return to see how our father will receive us, the grown sons he didn't raise, hasn't spoken to in ten years.

Love, Charley

To: Mom
From: Charley
Subject: Project Gold Rush
August 20, 2016

Dear Mom,

Here is a story Del told me when I was a boy about when he was a boy, about a thunderstorm that hit during his paper route, the velocity he created, his frantic pedaling through the deluge toward home. The storm gutters were backing up, the puddles trying to catch his tires, take him down, but he had skills, became one with his old Schwinn American. Just as he rounded the corner, lightning struck the metal of his han-dlebars. Del said the world went TV-fuzzy, static framing a

black-and-white image of his street, his house, like he needed
to adjust the rabbit ears of his brain. Del said he never did fall,
that he made it home and dried himself off and the world kept
orbiting the sun, the moon kept orbiting the earth, the aliens
kept sending envoys to all three.

Did Del tell you this story? Is this why you loved him?
What was lovable about him?

Del saw his first ghost that night, his first alien abduction
happened not long after. The lightning electrified Del, marked
him. The lightning made Del a hero to the boy I was. And I
maybe have seen him like that since, not actually seeing him
with my physical eyes, perpetually awestruck. In my imagination, Del is more mythic than human, but really, Del died
sometime between his writing the note and our arrival at the
mine.

Del's fourth wife Brandy said he was killed by a collapsed
wall of cloudy magnesite, rocks like thin milk, like altostratus clouds, and turquoise blue mcguinnessite, rocks the color
of your eyes, of Chris's, in the federal mining claim Del and
Brandy purchased at the bottom of the recession in 2009.
When she told us we could go down and pay our respects,
Chris snorted. *Respect for what?*

Brandy says they couldn't retrieve his body, but that this is
what Del wanted, to be buried in the mine. *I think he expected to
expire first of all, though, not be killed and buried at the same time*, she
said. She and her sons, our half-brothers, made a grave site by
arranging a series of milky-white magnesite pieces in a heart
shape just to the left of the mine entrance. The boys were at
work, she told us, laying sod in town.

She handed me a crumpled piece of notepaper that she says
Del wrote as a last will and testament. Fully uncrumpled, it is
one sentence long: *The feds don't need to know nothing about this.*

It's the same handwriting that's in our note from Del, but when Chris showed Brandy our note she frowned at him.

That ain't from Del, she said.

Who else would have written it? Chris asked.

That part ain't my problem.

Here is what the website says Thomas Edison says, in his autobiography, about the afterlife:

> *Now, I don't make any claims whatever to prove that the human personality survives what we call "death." All I claim is that any effort caught by my apparatus will be magnified many times, and it does not matter how slight is the effort, it will be sufficient to record whatever there is to be recorded. Frankly, I do not accept the present theories about life and death.*

Thomas Edison sold mass-produced cement houses to the American public, but he could not design a device that could hear the dead, nor did he try to design a device that could listen to the trapped thoughts of mothers suffering dementia. I have an iPhone in my pocket, spend my days writing code, utilizing design software. Del's family uses an outhouse next to a chicken coop that has maybe a dozen skinny hens scratching around in it. They haul water in once a week in a giant cistern tank on a rickety old trailer. The propane tank has gone rusty. The mining claim is played out, historically stingy. It gave nothing to the original forty-niners. It was picked over again during the Great Depression and abandoned by 1948, the year the Edison branch of the Detroit Public Library opened in a rented storefront overlooking the expressway. Del overlooked the children of his first marriage for years, and then he died before he could look any of us in our eyes, most of which are the color of the mcguinnessite that buried him.

Love, Charley

To: Mom
From: Charley
Subject: Project Gold Rush
August 21, 2016

Mom, sod for commercial jobs is delivered by the pallet:

480 square feet of sod
8 foot rolls of Kentucky bluegrass
60 rolls per pallet in drought-tolerant, disease-resistant emerald blue

There are no specific industry recommendations for watering sod in the first few days. Only it has to be kept evenly moist until rooted. It takes careful monitoring and attention and should probably require a full Army Corps Environmental Impact Statement on the effects of the water table in Tonopah, Nevada.

Each of those sod rolls weighs at least thirty pounds, and to see them carried, two at a time, on the wiry shoulders of a fourteen-year-old boy shocked my heart electric like Del's handlebar lightning.

The sod supervisor leaned close to our young half-brother, who pulled back, threw up his hands, and yelled: *I'm just trying to do a good job.*

The supervisor squared his shoulders, pointed at the boy's chest. *You're getting paid by the square foot, not by the good job.*

Another boy, unmistakably related, stood up behind the first, yelled at the supervisor. *Turn green, jackass.*

Chris tugged at the elbow of my shirtsleeve. His other hand was spread open over his heart, his eyes welling. *Mom*, he said, his voice strangling in his tears.

Did you give Del your *turn green* insult? Or did he give it to you?

Thomas Edison spent two years pursuing domestic rubber horticulture with Henry Ford and Henry Firestone (who share initials and inventive automotive fortunes, just like Chris and me) in his lab in West Orange, New Jersey, and in his home in Florida. The New York Botanical Society records show that seventeen thousand plant specimens were gathered from across the southern US, the best a hybridized goldenrod that yielded 12 percent rubber.

I am rubber. Chris is glue. He wants to keep the Tonopah family. He wants to raise them, shelter them, rub the balm of caretaking all over his grief. I'm not surprised by grief, with your illness gone so severe, and now, suddenly, Del. I carry my own share of it around, but I recognize that the weight of Chris's grief is somehow mine multiplied, grief to the power of near unbearable.

Our oldest half-brother, Colton, is fifteen, twenty-six years younger than me. Michael is fourteen. When they saw our note from Del, Colton embraced us both.

You have his eyes, Colton said, looking at me.

When we returned to the mine, Colton invited us in for coffee without asking Brandy's permission.

You enter the—it's not a house really, more of a dwelling—through a wooden lean-to, graying boards that shift, entirely, to the left, then open into a cave cut into the side of the mountain itself. It seems like it might have been a staging room for

the old-timey miners, a company office. There are two sets of
bunk beds that seem to have been hand-built from pallet wood,
a woodstove next to a propane camp stove. A large gun safe
sits next to a ceramic utility sink. There's no running water, but
they've plumbed the drains with PVC pipe out a crack in the
lean-to and into a ditch outside. In the middle of the room is a
solid wood table with four chairs, dusty maps and quitclaim
deeds and notices covering its surface.

Michael struck a match, lit the propane stove, made the
coffee. When I opened the envelope of powdered creamer, it
spilled all over Colton's hand-drawn map of the mine. Brandy
sucked her teeth at me.

There is one thing about planting sod. Not all soil amend-
ments are created equal. To water strength down into the
root system, to build drought tolerance and break up any
hardpan earthen layers under the soil crust, add phospho-
rus. For general good health, joy, and transmission capacity,
the savvy gardener will emphasize potassium over nitrogen. I enjoy bananas; the deep majestic purple dinner-plate
"Thomas Edison" dahlia enjoys Miracle-Gro. Del's Tonopah
family is just like Del, all three of them. They seek the flash
and sparkle of a nitrogen infusion—something that makes
them showier, more obviously golden, more present in the
world.

Colton and Michael have promised to take Chris and me
into the mine tomorrow. We will have to be careful about what
we promise in return.

                                        Love, Charley

To: Mom
From: Charley
Subject: Project Gold Rush
August 22, 2016

I didn't follow them past the timber-framed entrance to the
mine. I've seen more welcoming caves in my life, Mom. This
mine breathes the barometric wind, seeks to balance pressure.
During storms, this mine whispers mythic quest stories—
something about desire, about fallibility—or maybe the mine
is its own Frank's Box, and it's Del whispering, but it's either
nonsense, or Esperanto, or Tlingit, or another language in
which I can't communicate fluently.

When you pass on, maybe I'll lease a mining claim, wait for
the cave to start whispering.

Chris came out of the mine leaking whispered secrets. Two
years ago, he spent ten thousand dollars on court fees for a half-
sister we have in Reno, Del's daughter by his second wife, who
got picked up on an identity theft charge. She lost her appeal
and is currently in a minimum-security prison in Colorado.
Chris writes her letters, sends Louis L'Amour paperbacks. Last
year, two other half-brothers, from Del's third wife in Detroit,
contacted Chris. They asked for tuition money to complete their
automotive training certificates, and when he sent it, they cut
contact. He paid a private investigator five thousand dollars to
discover that they had embezzled money from a charter school,
skipped bail, and taken jobs on a fishing tender outside Haines,
Alaska, under assumed names.

Chris has an impeccable instinct for businesspeople, but a
blind spot, or maybe a soft spot, for half-family. He didn't tell
me, he said, because the price of the new family was insignificant,

but he couldn't accurately calculate the costs of my disapproval.

Chris came out of the mine with new conviction about ownership of circuses and monkeys, apples and trees. He calculated the relative strength of wind from the south and from the west, the breathy through-line of generations. He will not return to LA without the boys, and they won't leave the mine without Brandy.

Did you find Del down there? I asked.

It's just a big pile of rocks, he said. *Obstructing everything.*

Colton is right. My eyes are unmistakably from Del, brown, unremarkable, focused best on the periphery. I don't want to believe my heart is from Del too, suspicious, wandering, beating so much for the search that it forgets to love what it has already found. I want a heart that loves easily and well, a heart so welcoming and resilient and good that it doesn't have to fear breaking. A heart like Chris's. A heart like yours.

Love, Charley

To: Mom
From: Charley
Subject: Project Gold Rush
August 23, 2016

Dear Mom,

We promised to retrieve the gun safe and the guns in the near future. We promised to stop in Las Vegas so Brandy could visit her sister. We took rooms at Circus Circus, more amusement park than casino. Our new brothers are children, after all, and Chris loves trapeze artists and tumblers. I felt we were gambling enough.

When Thomas Edison was fifteen, he traveled around the

country filling in as a telegraph operator for men gone to fight the Civil War. Those were electric years for young Edison, years of transmission, of formation, of meaning-making. Our half-brothers spent hundreds of Chris's dollars on the midway at Circus Circus, throwing basketballs at a tilted hoop until they won a life-sized stuffed bear for their mother.

The plan was to meet at the Prius at 7 a.m., get an early start. The sun was firmly up when Chris and I walked out, blinding where it reflected off the metal and glass of the Strip. Later, we watched security footage of Brandy and the boys, with a stolen set of keys, driving away at 3 a.m. Colton was behind the wheel, Brandy in the front seat, Michael in the back with the giant bear.

It's nothing we can't afford, Chris said, shrugging.

We had taken the boys to watch the free circus acts, watched a woman in a polar bear leotard lie down on her back and juggle clear plastic ice cubes with all four limbs. Chris tried to explain that hydraulic engineering sought to amplify the power of human muscle, that someday he would find a way to make the jerky, stop-and-go hydraulic effect as elegant as the motion of the polar bear woman, of the tumblers. *The world could use more grace*, he said.

Later, Michael did flips into the outdoor pool. Colton teased him. *Graceful amplification! Elegant hydraulics!*

Chris cheered, refused to correct their Science.

Upon discovery of the empty parking space, Chris's face revealed something close to recognition. I wanted to call the police, but he smiled and pulled Del's will from his pocket: *The feds don't need to know nothing about this.*

We tabled our disagreement for discussion at a less emotional time and rented a car for the drive back to LA. The desert glowed pink, the soil reflecting the fading burn of a sky.

Chris and Chris's phone were both silent, and then Chris said, *We did what we could. I wish them well.*

I don't know exactly what to wish, Mom, but I thought about the way the wind sometimes blows the clouds lenticular over the mountains. Those clouds are the shape of lenses, named for lenses, but those clouds, like so many other things, are always opaque.

Love, Charley

Chickens

—

JUST BEFORE SMITH, THAT turncoat of an Agricultural
Extension agent, showed up on my farm with the rest of them, me
and Jerry stuffed my chickens into wax-covered produce boxes
and threw them in the back of the truck. I had just shy of a dozen
hens, plus Hitchcock, the rooster. We covered them with insulated
blankets to keep the noise down, and we played it real cool while
Smith and the other agents searched the place. Extension used to
be all advice and suggestion, but they're armed now, the agents, so
now it's more like monitoring and enforcement.

"I know you still have those birds, Gracie," Smith said, the toe
of his boot kicking open a fresh piece of chicken shit. "I've never
known you without chickens. Why not just cooperate?" Smith
looked awful smug for a guy who had soaked through the armpits of his shirt. I swear I couldn't believe, right then, that I'd ever
shared his bed.

Last month Congress banned outdoor poultry flocks on account
of the bird flu, made keeping chickens a Class A felony worth ten

years, minimum. An hour ago, my neighbor Fran called to warn us when Extension showed up at her house. Fran is a sweet white-haired lady who made a deathbed promise to my mother that she'd look after me, but mostly she just knits me a hat every Christmas. Fran's birds didn't have bird flu and neither did mine, but Extension was going house to house slaughtering any chicken that even maybe could have touched a wild bird. They didn't test them or anything. Raising chickens is regulated now. You need to lock them inside giant barns, install special ventilation and filters, pay for licenses and inspectors. Only millionaires can have chickens now.

I'm real attached to my chickens, the hens anyway. They're barred rocks, and they have the loveliest black-and-white patterns, not quite speckled but not quite striped either, with bright red heads and combs. Each one has its own shades and markings, which is something you couldn't tell unless you'd spent a lot of time with barred rocks the way I have. It's like what they say about snow-flakes and fingerprints. Each one of my girls is only ever just like herself.

I named my top hen Montana because her markings are just like the section of Rocky Mountain range that I can see, on clear days, from all the way out here. That range looks just like a woman lying on her back, knees bent, ready to take a lover, the peaks of her face raised to the sky, joyful and laughing, her hair all swept behind her into a shallow valley. Montana has those same peaks and val-leys etched right on her back, like God held her up and traced the pattern to get it exactly right. Sometimes I wonder whether God repeated beauty like that everywhere on purpose, like maybe he hoped humans would learn to see and reflect it, to find a way to copy it in the things we make ourselves. God is probably so disappointed.

"Hey buddy," Jerry said, looking at one of the agents. "Smith here, your big boss man, is having visions, thinks he's got some kind of psychic chicken second sight. You ought to make some kind of report about that."

Jerry was shirtless and the bottom of his pockets were hanging out under the frayed edges of his jean cutoffs, flapping against his legs. I hate those cutoffs. I tell him all the time those cutoffs are too short, but Jerry says he needs ventilation to keep his balls from getting swampy in the summertime, and I hate swampy balls, so there's that. He's six foot something, skeleton thin. He's got a bald spot on top but the rest of his hair is almost as long as his beard, which touches his chest even when he's staring straight ahead. Not a looker, but he sticks close by, so he'll do.

"Watch it, Jerry," Smith said. "I stay here long enough, I'll find those birds. This is an illegal chicken facility you're running. New rules say you build them a special shed or you don't raise them up anymore. It's for their own good. For the good of everybody. Can't be too careful with this bird flu thing."

"Jesus, Smith," I said. "Next you'll come tell me that you have to lock all the people up inside sheds. For their own good. To keep safe. Is that what you want?" I know my history; I believe the government is capable of that, maybe even eager. The worst part of it, I think, would be the vicious establishment of the human pecking order inside the shed itself.

Smith stared at me for a long time then, but he only shrugged, and he didn't find the birds.

"You better get these weeds taken care of, Grace," Smith said as he got in his truck, waving at my corral. That corral is a mess of puncture vine and Russian thistle since they took the water, with purple loosestrife blooms infesting the edges of my old irrigation ditch. "You know I have to report them."

"Spray them yourself if you want," I said. "The government is the only invasive weed I worry about these days."

I worried for a while after Smith drove off, a plume of red dirt rising off the road behind him, about calling the government an invasive weed. They say we still have free speech, but it's hard to tell for real anymore.

ME AND SMITH WERE sweethearts in high school and for a couple years after, but he ended up on the government side of the water grab a couple years ago, and that was the end of that. He's good-looking though. A lot better-looking than Jerry. Smith's looks are the only thing I know for sure about him anymore.

The water grab was hard to swallow because I was raised patriotic. My dad fought in Afghanistan and other places he wouldn't name. Growing up, I spent Memorial Day at cemeteries, not barbecues, thinking about how freedom ain't free. I touch my heart when I sing the national anthem. I remember at least half the 4-H pledge, too, and I take it serious, something about using my head and hands for the good of my country. I believed so much in democracy and liberty and such that the first time I heard someone say that the government was going to eminent-domain our water rights, I thought it was a dangerous rumor and I said so.

My acreage had so much water attached I could never use it up, on account of my great-great-grandfather was one of the first with enough imagination to replace the eastern Colorado scrub plains with sugar beets and feed corn. I could have turned my property into a private lake, learned to jet ski. I didn't, because corn was easy to grow and a whole lot quieter than a pissy little two-stroke engine, but I could have. Then drought, panic. Public opinion was firmly in favor of stealing my water rights. Everyone who didn't own water thought that folks who did, like me, were greedy, hoarding bastards.

Smith was in charge of the grunt crew installing locks on the irrigation headgates that day. Fran's farm and mine shared a junction box, and I took my cues from her—chin up, back straight, eyes on everything, unblinking. The director of Extension, supervising Smith's crew, seemed unsettled by our presence. We could see his eyes looking our way even though he didn't turn his head.

Fran turned to me, shielding her eyes from the sun with one hand. "You know this was coming? He tell you?" The men could all hear her. She meant Smith, and I could tell he knew it because he went as red as he had the first time he saw me shirtless back when we were both just sixteen.

"Seems like he should have," I said. Smith and I had woken up together that morning, swearing at Hitchcock's incessant crowing, but out in the field he wouldn't meet my eyes. It was like I was holding the scales of justice. On one side, I put the corsage he'd gotten me for our senior prom, the earrings I knew weren't real diamonds but sparkled like they were, the promises he'd whispered, as I sobbed in his arms at my mother's funeral, that he'd take care of me. At the time, I'd taken his stone-faced solemnity for strength, but there, as he helped the government steal my water, I put it on the other side of the scale—stone face, stone heart—and I knew he and I had lost any sense of balance.

Fran frowned. "It does seem that way. Unless, of course, this is his way of telling you something else, Gracie."

The director of Extension gave Smith a hard look. Smith stared into the junction box, and I was glad to realize he was seeing a warped reflection of himself down there, the water disturbed by the action of the lock installation.

Most farmers out here put up more of a fight than me and Fran, of course, but Extension, with the National Guard on their side, made short work of the standoff. In related news, nobody cares that I can't put crops in the ground without water, that my savings are near used up and my taxes are near due. Bacon grows in petri dishes now, corn comes husked and wrapped in clear plastic. People don't care about farmers unless it's Halloween and they're looking to visit a pumpkin patch.

Hiding these chickens is real founding fathers shit. Straight justified civil disobedience. Anyone paying attention knows that birds belong outside. Seagulls follow the plows. Eagles glide on the high winds. Geese in V-formation still migrate with the seasons. Besides, you have to be exposed to develop immunity. That virus might soar for miles on the prairie wind like seeds of milkweed, of blue flax, but so does the dust that scours our noses and ears, the sunshine that bleaches us clean. My girls and their line will outlive those shed birds by a thousand years. They won't have to be afraid of wind and sunshine, of seagulls and seeds.

I'm ashamed it took me two weeks after the headgate incident to kick Smith off my farm, because every time he touched me it felt like he was stealing something else, but I have appetites, if you know what I mean. One reason Jerry's here is that I can't abide having a cold spot in bed. For a long time, I've been hoping I'll start to love Jerry the same way I loved Smith. Jerry is a better man, softhearted, which is new for me and I like it. Jerry's kindness opens me all up inside, blows the stink right out of me. Jerry puts a bouquet on the breakfast table every morning, even when all he can find is milkweed or ditch sunflowers. He has strong opinions about the consumption of green leafy vegetables, makes us smoothies every morning and skillet greens for dinner. I never have to wonder whether Jerry's on my team, but I don't always know if I'm all the way on his.

THREE OF THE HENS smothered during that first Extension raid, but Hitchcock and Montana and the rest came out of it okay. I've been taking Fran eggs every day to thank her. That must be all she eats because every day I see her she's shrunk a little more.

I still have my garden, but she won't take any vegetables. She says they give her the slipperies.

My girl Montana is the top of the pecking order and she keeps the other hens in line. We keep them hidden behind the barn now, one wing clipped, the wire fence hidden from sight by the pigweed and lamb's-quarters, the Indian cabbage and ditch sunflowers I've let grow. They're all twined together, those weeds, their branches linked up like kids playing Red Rover, a wall solid enough to keep the hens hidden in place. I like to watch the flock scratch around and gossip. Those girls have opinions about everything. For example, they don't much care for their new covert lifestyle. They prefer things free-range. They think Hitchcock, the rooster, is a real jackass. I happen to agree.

Hitchcock is always strutting around like he owns the place, jumping those poor girls whenever he feels like it, which is all the time. He's insatiable. He tore the feathers right off poor Betty's back when he mounted her, which I think is why she's gone all broody and refuses to leave the clutch she's nesting on in the barn. The crowing isn't as much a problem as you'd think because Jerry made his living selling no-crow rooster collars to the backyard chicken crowd. It's real humane, the collar, just wire and Velcro around the rooster's neck. I wouldn't say this to Jerry but it's not really no-crow either. Hitchcock crows all day and all night. The collar keeps him just quiet enough that the neighbors don't hear, and at night I put a bushel basket overtop of him. We've got boxes and boxes of no-crow rooster collars in my hayloft because there's nobody to sell them to now. We're using Hitchcock to start our breeding program, and then eventually we'll need those collars for the little baby roosters our girls are going to hatch. We've already got a waiting list of people who want their own secret flock. Mostly they're last-minute preppers. They might be militia. Jerry's worried some of them might be government spies, but the truth about Jerry is that he's always been real paranoid.

One time we were driving through Nebraska, me and Jerry, and a cop pulled behind us in the lane. His lights weren't on or anything. Jerry got all worked up about a dime bag he'd stuffed in the ashtray before we left. He was mumbling some nonsense about redneck cops and the war on drugs. I wasn't speeding and I knew my taillights and blinkers and all the stupid stuff cops pull poor people over for were working. The only thing was my Colorado plates. Nebraska cops were still super pissed off about legal weed in Colorado back then. You had to be a little careful.

"We've got to get rid of this shit," Jerry said.

"Be cool," I told him. "We're fine."

I heard some rustling, and next thing I knew, Jerry had a mouthful of weed. He ate everything in the bag. I had to give him my Pepsi to keep him from choking on how dry it was. The cop got off the freeway two exits later.

Jerry's real sweet, but he's a lot to handle.

"THEY'RE COMIN' FOR THE damn chickens!" Jerry's eyes were all crazy, and he kept looking over his shoulder and waving his shotgun around. I have sometimes moaned about the plains, about no trees, no hills, no nothing but fields and ditches and short-grass prairie between me and the Rockies, the summer noon so hot I might melt, spread invisible-thin across the land, become tiny and helpless in the vast, big-sky world, but anyway the good part of it is the view is unobstructed. You can see deer rustling in a field five miles away. Behind Jerry, past the dry ditch, past the oil rigs, past Fran's house, I could see a line of red dirt plume rising, traffic on the road moving quick toward my farm.

I had the same feeling I got right before the first raid, like when I used to jump into the snowmelt rush of the South Platte in June. I couldn't fill my lungs. My arms were thrashing around but not doing anything specific. My blood felt thick and gummy, slowed way down while panic sped the rest of me up. The air, like the water, held me down, constrained me.

"Grace, this isn't a drill! Not a drill! Get to the bunker!" Jerry was shirtless again and barefoot, running across the corral all frantic, and then he must have stepped on a goathead or something because he started swearing and jumping up and down, staying in one spot but turning in a circle, holding the shotgun with one hand and grabbing at his foot with the other.

Jerry worked the goathead loose and started running toward me again. "Goddammit, Gracie, move!" he yelled. We had a plan for this contingency, and yes, we'd run a few drills. We'd built a chicken coop bunker out of pallets we stole from the feed store. We lined them with scraps of plywood and stuffed them with straw until we had real solid walls. We had ammo and jerky and bottled water and K-Y Jelly stored in there. We could hold off a raid for a good long time. I'm realistic, so I knew that if we drew guns on Extension, it probably wouldn't end well. Of course, I didn't really believe it would come to that.

The dust cloud was moving closer. Jerry was still yelling. I grabbed Montana and three or four other chickens by their legs, flipping them upside down. This is supposed to calm the birds, or at least trick them into holding still. My hens are a bunch of ingrates, so they flapped around, screeching, trying to get a piece of my hand, or a fingernail, with their beaks. Jerry caught the other hens and we got them into the barn coop. I ran for my .22 while Jerry chased after Hitchcock. A .22 is not much of a gun. It's embarrassing to bring a .22 to a standoff with the government, but I had to

live with the insult to my vanity. I climbed into the coop with the
hens and looked out the peephole.

"Goddammit, bird," Jerry said. He was half bent over, real ape-
like, trying to grab Hitchcock. "This is for your own damn good.
This is for the good of *humanity*."

My dad would have known better than me and Jerry what to
do. He was trained so well for combat he started to live for it, to
seek it everywhere, create it when he couldn't find it. I was real
mad at him when I was a girl, for re-enlisting all the time, for leaving me and Mom to grow the crops, manage the harvest, keep the
woodpile stocked all winter. Now that I've had some time to think
it through, I know he probably did it for our own good, because
he knew deep down we weren't the enemy even though he treated
us like we were most times. Still, I was real hateful to him the last
time I saw him, just after my eighteenth birthday, when he flew
home for Mom's funeral. He told me he had to go back, that he'd
used up all his leave. I told him if I wanted to see him I'd just join
the fucking jihad. I got the visit a few months later, the folded flag.
It's up in barn storage, covered in a bunch of no-crow collars.

Jerry worked up a sweat chasing Hitchcock around. His forehead dripped and glistened, and the moisture set random chunks
of his eyebrows against the grain. Hitchcock and Jerry were in a
standoff, Hitchcock in full choked little crow, when Smith came
through the barn door. I had a good view and a clear shot into that
scene. I chewed some jerky and settled in for whatever was going
to happen next.

Smith was dressed up fancy, and he had one hand behind his
back. His brown wingtips were huge, like real-life fancy clown
shoes. He had overstarched his button-down shirt, but it was blue
and it made his green eyes look good, and his blazer was only a little worn in the elbows. He looked real handsome even though his
mouth was gaping open all weird at Jerry. Smith couldn't see me.

He wouldn't have expected to find me in the chicken coop, wouldn't have recognized the bunker as a coop. I don't know if Smith saw Hitchcock because the rooster went frozen and still, but Smith and Hitchcock looked a lot alike in that moment. They both looked worried and their feet were planted in odd directions. The rooster's eye was moving, vigilant, watching the two men. Smith was keeping one eye on Jerry, taking the measure of things with the other.

"Grace around?" Smith asked.

Jerry pivoted his body between Smith and Hitchcock and pointed the shotgun at Smith. "I want to see your piece," Jerry said, real calm. "I want to know what you're holding."

Smith took a step back and put a hand up, but it was a one-handed surrender, like promising something with your fingers crossed. "Let's just calm down. I only came out to talk to Grace. I catch you at a bad time, Jerry?"

"Who else you got out there?" Jerry said, lunging the shotgun toward the door. Jerry's voice was like one of those old-timey crank sirens, getting louder, more shrill, by degrees. "You got the guard out there?"

Smith seemed genuinely confused. "Wha?" he said. "The guard? What guard?"

"The National fucking Guard!" Jerry hit full wail, hopping from one foot to the other. He looked like he was on drugs. It's possible he was on drugs. "I know you're too chickenshit to come alone!"

Hitchcock made his move from behind then, launching with a staccato, helicopter whoosh. His talons, the scaly genetic gift from his dinosaur ancestors, landed on Jerry's shoulder and he beat Jerry about the head with his wings, the triumphant battle crow reduced to a few pathetic squeaks by his no-crow collar. Jerry let out some real high-pitched whoops and shrieks. He twisted around trying to lose the rooster, finally leaping onto a stack of two hay bales. In the chaos, his gun went off and I saw the spray of blood when the bullet hit Smith, who after a little staggering collected himself enough to pull a gun of his own out of a concealed holster and fire two really impressive shots. He took out Hitchcock and Jerry both before he hit the ground, and then they were all three silent, motionless. Next to Smith, the loose dirt from the barn floor was swirling, floating paisley patterns on top of a seeping puddle of blood, and in the middle of that spread was a single white rose. I couldn't see Jerry.

I retched up my jerky. Montana and the other hens started right away to eat it, fighting each other for position around my gut's steamy offering. All except Betty, who stayed watchful on her nest, protecting the shell-encased embryos of an entire possible future. People think chickens are stupid, use "birdbrain" like it's some kind of insult, but my girls have an instinct for self-preservation. They come home to roost at night. They scatter when shadows appear in the sky, search for cover from chicken hawks and bald eagles. They go broody when they need to and sometimes when they don't, like they're getting in some maternity practice. Soon, there in the coop bunker, the vomit was gone and Montana sat in my lap, preening her feathers, while I breathed deep and regular, trying to calm down.

I was thinking I should make a call, but the only government-type person I'd halfway trust was lying dead on my barn floor. I assumed a massacre, of course. It's natural I thought that, seeing that I lost both my parents at a pretty tender age. I imagine that every age you lose a parent is tender, probably, no matter how old you are. It's a raw sort of feeling. It didn't occur to me that any of those boys were still alive until I heard the moaning.

"Grace?"

It was a thin whisper, was all. I could barely hear it. I checked to be sure my .22 was ready, and crawled out of the coop.

I went to check on Jerry first. I knelt next to him, not realizing right away that the cool, thick wet I felt wicking its way into my pant legs, spreading in all directions around my knees, was Jerry's blood. His breathing was ragged and shallow. I took the shotgun out of his hands, kissed his bald spot, and whispered, "I'm sorry, Jerry."

"My leg, Gracie."

Jerry was bleeding bad from a wound in his thigh, near his groin but, luckily, not into his delicates. I grabbed at a pile of oil-soaked rags near the old Farmall, and Jerry winced when I pushed down, trying to put some pressure on the wound. The oil wasn't perfect, probably, but those rags were all I had to stanch the bleeding.

"You all right, Jerry?"

"That bastard shot me."

"You shot first."

"Accident," Jerry said, and then he shuddered, and then he passed out. I made a tourniquet then, tight as I could. The blood slowed, but still it seeped and puddled into the folds of the oil rag, staining it further. I must have gotten a little lost in the image, because when I heard Smith call my name, I felt a chunk of time I could not quantify had fallen away from me.

"Grace," Smith whispered. I looked his way. One of his hands raised up off the floor and held still for a minute, like he was giving me a real casual wave hello. It confused me, that wave, like maybe he wasn't as hurt as he seemed, but when I got closer I could tell he was. His gun was still in his hand. He wasn't pointing it at me on purpose, but the angle made me nervous, so I gently reached over and took it from him.

"Smith?" I said. "What the hell are you doing here?"

Smith managed a weak smile. "Dying, I think."

"No."

"Maybe. I brought you a rose, Grace."

The rose was now fully immersed in a puddle of blood. When Smith picked it up and handed it to me, blood dripped off the tips and ran in warm, viscous rivulets down his hand and under the cuff of his fancy blazer.

"That's real nice of you, Smith."

"You want to have dinner sometime?"

"Sure, Smith, but first I'm going to get you and Jerry over to Fran's. She can help you."

"Fran was my piano teacher when I was a boy."

"Yes."

"I killed all her chickens. I didn't want to, Gracie. I know what you mean, that thing you said about sheds and people and fear. But I did it anyway. It was my job, and I did it."

"You sure did."

"Fran hates me now."

"Maybe." I hesitated for a minute. Smith wasn't wrong to worry that Fran might be holding a grudge, and I wondered if I should take him to the hospital instead. Jerry, too. Smith seemed sweet, repentant. He sounded like he was on my side, at least about the chickens. But what if he was just trying to soften me up so I'd show my hand? What if the rose was Smith's way of making sure I didn't best him on this chicken thing, a way to get me in bed before he took me to prison? Being caught with chickens was bad enough, but what would keep the police and Extension and God and everybody from thinking I was the one who shot them both? I'd just touched every gun in that barn. My fingerprints were everywhere.

I thought of all the questions, the police investigation, the ramped-up Extension enforcement, and I looked at my own girls, who had swarmed around Hitchcock and were working together to make a meal of him. Montana had torn open his back vent, and the girls were working on a full disembowelment, pulling on his intestines like gray-blue membrane-shiny maypole ribbons.

I was very fond of Smith, but I was not going to take any chances with the authorities. I took off my sweater, all the fabric I had, and piled it onto the bullet wound.

"Come on," I said. "Fran will know what to do."

"Fran was my piano teacher."

"Yes."

"Fran hates me."

"Probably."

I tried propping Smith up, having him lean on me but walk on his own power toward the truck, but it didn't work and he took me down with him. We landed all jumbled up together, my arm pinned under his ass, his left leg overtop of my right. It felt nice to be close to Smith, except it was alarming how light he felt, how loose and floppy his limbs were, the way the blood had started to soak into his wingtips. I am on the small side of average for a woman, but farm life has made it so that I can lift improbable things. I picked Smith up over my shoulders and carried him. He had parked me in, so I headed for his truck instead of mine. Letting him down turned out to be lots harder than picking him up. I tried to be gentle, but I stumbled when I opened the door and dropped him pretty hard into the passenger seat. He moaned some then. His keys were in his pocket, so I had to grope him some to get at them. He kept on moaning, his eyes turned up into his head like he was trying to read the fine print on his own brain.

I tried to move Jerry, too, but I had used myself all up. My arms and shoulders burned and shook. I just couldn't manage it. I propped him against a hay bale, kissed his cheek. He was still breathing.

"I'll be back, Jerry," I whispered, letting my lips move against the softness of Jerry's ear. "I'll send Fran."

Tears prickled the back of my eyes as I walked away from Jerry. I know I'm not the person I wish I was because even though me and Jerry had been together for a couple years, and even though he was always real nice to me and I cared about him a lot, I was happy it was Smith already in the truck.

FRAN CAME OUT TO meet us in her driveway. She had her white hair up in a bun held together by two lead pencils and was wearing a house apron that covered almost all of her, like a painting smock. Smith wasn't talking anymore, but he was bleeding a little slower than in the barn.

"Take him into the kitchen," Fran said, glancing over each shoulder at the road. "Keep him over the linoleum. I don't want him bleeding all over my rugs." Fran wasn't smiling but neither did she look particularly grim. It was hard to tell what she was thinking.

I laid Smith down, gentler this time, on Fran's floor. "You going to help him?" I asked.

"I'll look him over," she said, handing me an old towel, frayed at the edges, with holes where bleach had eaten through the terry cloth.

"Okay."

"Where's Jerry?"

"He's shot too. In the barn. Can you go?"

Fran nodded. "After I look to this one, I'll go." She pointed at Smith's truck. "You best go hose out that truck. Try and get the blood as close to the stock tanks as you can, in the tall grass behind the barn where we slaughter the beef cows. Then you get that truck inside that empty grain silo in the back pasture."

"Okay," I said. Fran's hair was impossibly neat, not a strand out of place. I wondered how she managed it with those pencils, thought I'd ask her sometime about her technique.

"Grace," she said. Her voice was sharp, like a slap. "You get that truck out of sight quick now. Quick, girl."

"Okay."

The earth swallowed Smith's blood, the grass covering everything. The silo smelled sweet, fermented, like cider. I walked back to the house. Fran came out with a bundle of linens. She threw her bundle and the towel I'd used in her burn barrel, doused them with diesel, and lit the whole thing up. I stood there for a minute, mesmerized by the flames and the fumes, trying to get my head to focus, to formulate some sort of plan. The fire was not part of a holiday, not a summer celebration. This was not the end. There was still the coop, and Jerry, and whatever was left of Hitchcock.

"Jerry?" I asked.

"He's okay. Got him bandaged up and comfortable. Needs the hospital soon, but that's not your biggest problem, girl."

"Smith is going to die?"

"Ha!" Fran laughed. It was musical, like someone hit the middle C. "Dead men tell no tales. Darling, your problem is that this one is going to live."

"Is he awake? Like is he talking right now?"

"No." Fran was holding her hands over the fire, even though it was plenty warm outside. "Does anyone know he was at your place?"

"Not sure. He brought me a rose, is all. Asked me to dinner."

Fran gave me a long stare, right in my eyes. "Did he see your birds?"

"Yes."

"Jerry shot first?"

"Yes."

Fran shook her head. "Gracie," she said, "you have to make some decisions."

"What should I do?" I asked. Fran, all sweet and white-haired on the outside, with her piano lessons and her knitting needles, just stared at me.

"You do what you want," she said, "but listen. I'm going to burn my slash pile tonight. You got anything needs burning, I can throw it on."

Fran was like Montana. Beautiful. Nurturing. Ruthless.

I shook my head and went inside. It wasn't the first time I'd thought of killing a man. I'd thought about it a lot the times my dad was home from war, whiskey-clumsy, talking down my mom and me. It didn't seem likely that I'd pull it off, though, especially not with Smith. Then again, Smith had stolen my water, come for my chickens. This shit now was just the after-that of both those things, an ending that was starting to feel heavy, inevitable. My dad told me once that no matter how much he believed in spreading democracy and just wars and retribution for terrorists, it still took everything he had to look at another human through the sight of his gun, a body with a beating heart, with people who loved and were loved by them, a life in progress, and pull the trigger.

"In the end, Gracie," he'd said, "you do it because you're scared shitless that they'll shoot you first."

Fran's kitchen smelled mostly like applesauce but also metallic, like Smith's blood. Smith's head was shaved, his clothes were rumpled, and a thin line of drool ran out of the corner of his mouth. On his blazer, stuck to the lapel, was a piece of chicken down. I didn't know if it came from Hitchcock or Montana, but the wispy tendrils were shivering as Smith's chest rose and fell. Next to him, on the floor, lay a wooden-handled kitchen cleaver.

I wanted to feed him. I wanted to bite him. I wanted to smash my boot in his nose.

I couldn't stop thinking of the day they came to take the water, years ago, when Smith just stood there, head shaved, gun drawn, pretending not to know me as the director of Extension locked my water away. I closed my eyes, trying to picture Smith the way I had loved him best, back when we were both just high school kids and everything was still real simple. At our senior prom, his rented tux fit him perfectly. He wore his hair long and his curls caught my fingers as I straddled him in the backseat of his mother's car. I can still picture the way the full moon gave a sheen to the vinyl upholstery, the oily flavor of Smith's Altoids coating my own tongue.

Back in Fran's kitchen, I needed my rage, but somehow I couldn't muster it. I closed all the windows. It helped to feel confined, penned in, to want for fresh air. I knelt next to Smith, the linoleum cool on my shins. I wrapped my left fingers around the knife handle, ran my right knuckles along the side of his cheek. He smiled a little in his sleep. I leaned in close, ran my tongue along the curved edge of his ear.

"What," I whispered, my lips moving against the soft fuzz on his skin, "did you mean with that rose?"

Smith shifted a little, laid his entire forearm along the length of my thigh. He didn't open his eyes, and he didn't answer my question. I thought of Jerry, the way he used to put my braids between his thumb and his forefinger, run his fingers up and down them, declare his love for them, for me. He did the same thing with loose chicken feathers when he listened to the radio. Jerry said repetitive actions helped him get in touch with himself. I felt the steady beat of Smith's life where his skin warmed mine, and I breathed again, deep and regular, trying to match my pulse to his, trying to get in touch with myself. I was not afraid to act in my own best interest, but I could no longer discern the correct action. My instincts had lost clarity, cut to static. I imagined murderer's prison, chicken-keeper's prison. I saw my fields parched, my coop empty, my nation as confused and chaotic as my own silly girl heart—aching for freedom that seeps ever away, watching liberty puddle outside itself. Like tears. Like blood.

Acknowledgments

—

I am lucky to be part of a giant extended family with a history of shenanigans and a collective gift for storytelling. I learned from the masters, and I am grateful to every last one of you. For the stories in this book, I want to thank especially my Granny Ruth, my Grandma Aunt Mano, Father Al, and my aunts Marcia, Sue, and Cathy (the original three sisters). Also, my uncle Don, my aunts Barb, Kate, and Lisa, and my cousins Eva and Sally, who have always made space in their lives for art and science and family and love all at once, which is how I learned it was possible.

My parents, Dave and MaryAnne, taught me to hold on to joy no matter what else I have to carry, and to try to be patient, which is to say that they taught me how to be a writer and a human.

My brother, Zac, is a master of balancing serious drama with lighthearted good humor, in writing and in real life. Our friendship is a centering force and I would not be whole without it.

My sister, Maggie, is the most caring and competent of any of us and has never once been afraid to call out my bullshit, which I will admit (just this once, in this space only) has made me a better person.

Thank you to Dick and Bonnie and every member of the extended Boyles family for accepting me into the fold and introducing me to the delights of a beach house vacation.

Kate Garrick, my agent, made all of this happen while being delightfully funny and supportive, even as the world took a turn, so I'm certain that she is a magical human. I am also grateful to Cathy Jaque and everyone at the Karpfinger Agency.

Jill Bialosky, Drew Elizabeth Weitman, and everyone at W. W. Norton helped me find new depths in these stories. Thank you all so much for deciding to take a chance on my work.

At Colorado State, Judy Doenges, Camille T. Dungy, Deborah Thompson, EJ Levy, Andrew Altschul, and Leslee Becker were wonderfully engaged and supportive teachers. Nic Brown encouraged my fiction in some very early bumpy stages, and Vauhini Vara's incredibly generous journalism lessons have been useful in creative nonfiction and fiction both.

I am grateful to everyone involved in organizing and executing both the Bread Loaf Orion Environmental Writers' Conference and the Community of Writers. I feel very lucky to have been able to attend those programs. The residency I received from the Kimmel Harding Nelson Foundation was an incredible gift of time and quiet. To everyone at the *Kenyon Review*, the *Masters Review*, *Boulevard*, *VQR*, and other journals that have published my work, thank you, especially David Lynn, Kirsten Reach, Kim Winternheimer, Allison Wright, and Dusty Fruend. Alexander Chee's encouragement and support have also been incredibly important.

My Colorado State MFA classmates—fiction, poetry, and

CNF—are the smartest and best, all of you. You let me join your lovely nonsense without ever making me feel old and ridiculous, and you read everything with generosity and kindness and wit. Thanks especially to Emily Ziffer, Emily Harnden, Cory Cotten-Potter, Sam Killmeyer, David Mucklow, Michelle Thomas, Caleb Gonzalez, and Melissa Merritt. Also, everyone in Nic Brown's graduate fiction class at UNC and the writing group that grew out of it, especially Ty Cronkite, Cameron Markway, and Jonnie Genova, and to Mary Scalise and her book club here in Loveland, who provided helpful feedback.

My workshop groups at Community of Writers and BLO, especially Victoria Blanco, Megan Tucker Orringer, Leslieann Hobayan, Lupita Eyde-Tucker, Re Marzullo, Holly LaBarbera, and Sabrina Sarro.

Meghan Pipe and Debbie Vance read approximately eight million drafts of these stories and gave thoughtful and detailed feedback on every single one. They check in regularly with my writing and my heart and send chocolate and booze when necessary. I'd be lost without either of them, in writing and in life.

Jim Myers generously let me tag along while he shared what he knew about ditches and water and sugar mills and the world, and I'm happy to have him as a friend.

Jaymi Anderson, Holly Collingwood, Harmony and Bill Tucker, John and Mary Poor, Peg and Ed Sanders, Nic Koontz and Katie Slota, Darci Hata and Ian Mickells, Leanne Porzycki, Katja Nix, Dan Hotch, Dan Park, Paris Hunt, John Morrissey, Luke Vance, and everyone else who makes my life happy and rich—thanks for staying on my team for all these years, friends.

My husband, Matty, to whom this book is dedicated, did all the housework and everything else for years so that I could write these stories in stolen hours before and after work, all while helping me see the best of myself. Thank you for sharing this life with me.

And finally, most urgently, to Madzie and Simon, two fierce, brilliant, passionate humans about to launch their own beautiful lives. This crazy world is lucky to have you, and so am I. All my love, forever.